THREE NOVELLAS

THREE NOVELLAS

Cameron H. Chambers

iUniverse, Inc.
Bloomington

THREE NOVELLAS

iUniverse books may be ordered through booksellers or by contacting:

iUniverse
1663 Liberty Drive
Bloomington, IN 47403
www.iuniverse.com
1-800-Authors (1-800-288-4677)

ISBN: 978-1-4620-4629-4 (sc)
ISBN: 978-1-4620-4630-0 (ebk)

Printed in the United States of America

iUniverse rev. date: 08/25/2011

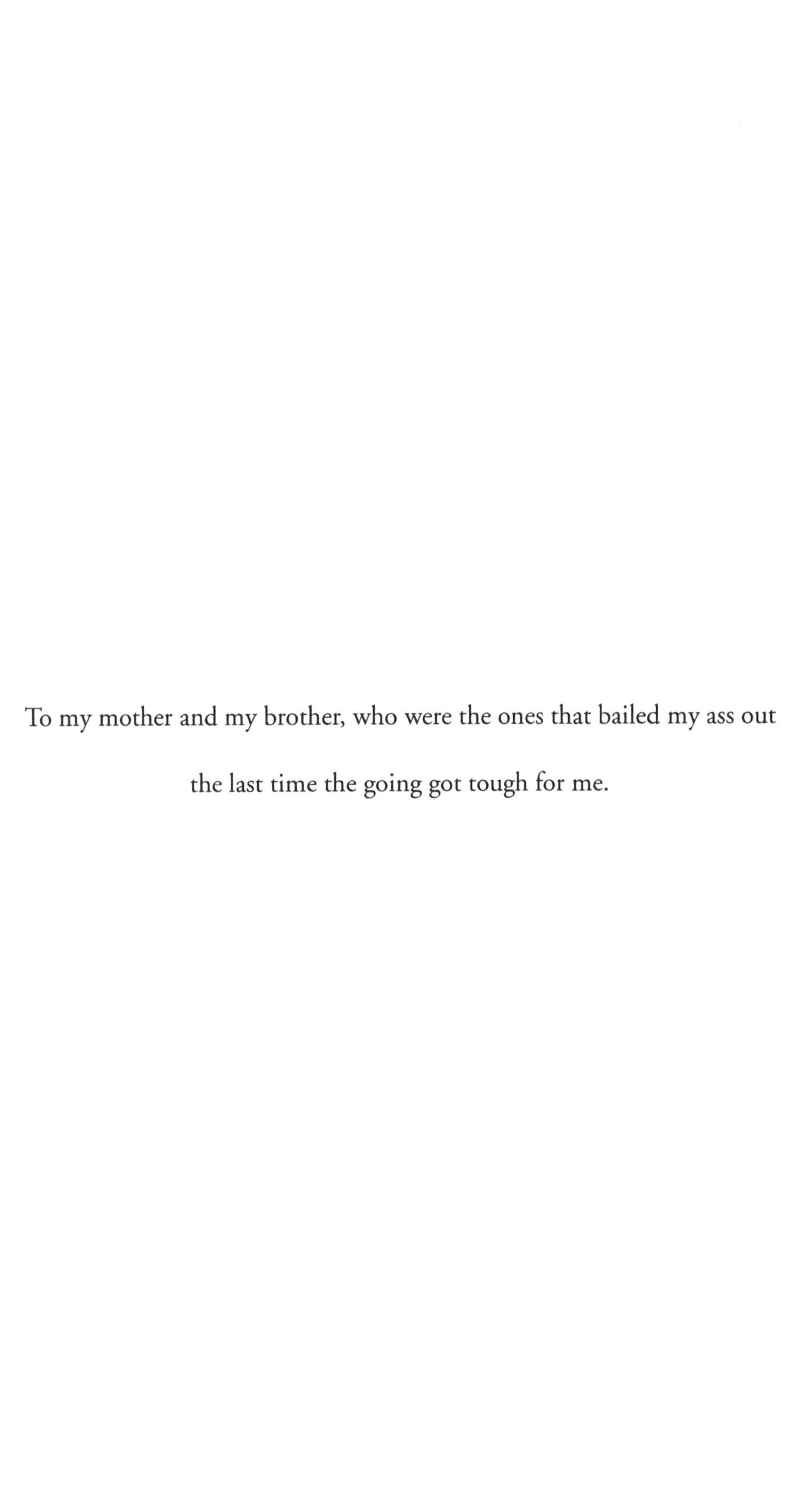

To my mother and my brother, who were the ones that bailed my ass out

the last time the going got tough for me.

The Revelation of Chris Devin

A Novella

By

Cameron H. Chambers

Also by Cameron H. Chambers:

Don't Cross the Devil

Confessions of an Internet Don Juan

The Stone Cabin

For the Love of a Madman

www.cameronhchambers.com

Chapter One

Hi, I am Chris Devin. I am an Internet Don Juan, but that's another story and I went by another name. I have been divorced twice, had my nose broken three times, been beaten up a half dozen times, attempted suicide twice; I was homeless for two years, filed bankruptcy once, and had four major psychoses. I was also raped as a child on more than one occasion. Oh, and I am an alien. The space alien kind. Like the Coneheads, but not from France. I am an American. I am also the only person who has walked on the moon. Sorry, Neil Armstrong et al.

Allow me to reiterate. I am the only person who has walked on the moon. That was my biggest distinction for years, and I could not tell anyone, because I would have been locked up then. I consider myself a man, but my mom would probably say otherwise. I am only fifteen in this part of my saga. This saga will span about thirty years of my life. I was ten at the time I walked on the moon, but I still considered myself a man even then. I'll reflect on those years later. I was reborn during the Slick Willie Clinton boom years, and learned about Neil Armstrong and the others in history class. I thought it hysterically funny. There are plenty of people, mostly older conspiracy theorist types I know, that believe the moon launch was media hype, but I figured out how to get there and I was actually sent there by the CIA. There was a munitions depot on the moon, a gathering of ammo to be used in an invasion of earth. Someone had to blow it up and hopefully make it home again, which I did. It was a miracle I performed. I am a Saint, but I don't feel like one. I don't particularly behave like one either.

I am a typical kid though. I smoke pot occasionally, play soccer, basketball and baseball, and have a girlfriend named Sarah. She's got ginger hair and a ginger complexion, and I think she is incredibly beautiful, but she always disagrees when I tell her so. She's kind of strict with me some times, but I love her and I can't imagine being without her. We haven't had sex yet, but then the prom is not far off. I am a junior, but I get to go anyway. I started first grade when I was five. I go to a ritzy high school on the west side. My family can't afford it, but the school's headmaster finally gave me an academic scholarship, because he knew I was going places. I already own three patents for junk I invented. One has to suck up to those future infamous alums.

But he doesn't know anything about what I did. It was before I went to his school. Knowledge of my triumph was on a need-to-know basis only and that meant primarily the CIA. No one at my school knows. I don't know anyone who does know, or if the ones who did are still alive. You are probably wondering what kind of vehicle or rocket ship got me there, but it wasn't anything like that. I simply projected. Some mystical types, I have read, call it astral projection, but me, I just call it projection. It's simpler. My entire family knows I claim I do these things, but I get the sense they don't really believe me or care that much. To them, I am their kid brother who takes out the garbage and drinks the last soda.

I don't care either. I do it at night when I sleep. My dad knows the real story, and it's classified, but I felt like spilling my guts after all. I am kind of a maverick that way. I was ten when I landed on the moon. I said that already, but it bears repeating. This is the first time I ever told anyone. My dad, who was a high ranking military officer, and military intelligence knows the story, but my dad won't discuss it with me. I don't remember all that well what it was I did. It is like that for me when I astral project. I only sort of remember some of the places I have been. Many of them were fabulous, much prettier than earth.

My dad divorced my mom because the first born died. His name was Rob for short or Robert. I am Chris. My surviving brother is Al and my sister is Maggie. That is probably the last time I will mention their names because they play a very small role in this narrative. I'll skip around a lot too, and when I got older, my family had already fragmented because of the death of Robert, so it is very possible this narrative will seem very disjointed. Art mimics life, or vice versa. It could just be I am rather scattered.

My parents could not work it out together, so afterwards on my fourth birthday, my dad slipped out the door one night; he went out for a pack of cigarettes and I never saw him again, except once for a short time. My parents had had a huge fight. I remember my mom saying, "you'll wake Chris." The baby's room was right next door, and I was the baby. I knew what was going on even at age four. I was already awake. I cried. I heard the door slam. My dad wrote me in a letter once never to tell anyone what I had done because the KGB is always looking for news items like this. They would want to recruit me or abduct me. The KGB is the infamous Russian spy ring. I don't care. I want to be a journalist, so I need to begin somewhere. So this account is as good a place as any to begin.

I was told by someone very early in my life I was a saint and would do a miracle. He was a little Japanese man I met in Japan while traveling with my father. That was the one time I saw him again. My father, I mean. I am American as I have said. And I was just a young boy in Japan. The latest Pope decreed that to be considered a saint now, the saint has to perform two miracles. That's a pretty tall order, but then I guess a single miracle could be easily misinterpreted. I don't question the Pope in case he is right, even though I am not Catholic. I sometimes wish I was. Sarah is Catholic. Catholic people always seem to have good jobs.

I don't really care about being a saint. It has little to do with who I am. I am a kid. An ordinary kid. I ride my bike to my girlfriend's house. I have dinner with her family. Ordinary stuff. My opinion didn't change until one fateful day.

I was having dinner with my mom and my stepfather. He was boozing it up as usual, and he had made some off-hand remark that made me cry. I was kind of a sensitive kid—still am. I pushed away from the table and went up to my room. I don't remember what the remark was: something insensitive that a drunk might say. He had been very good to me though, but the toll of living with my mother was telling on him. He drank more and more. My mom hated men. My sister does too. I guess it was because my father walked out on my mom and three kids. My mom was devastated from the loss of Robert, the first born, and had never worked a day in her life, at least not at a paid job, until she got divorced. And then all of a sudden she was a single mom with three kids. She kind of lost her humanity. It's understandable in a way. There are five in our household—I live with my brother and sister and my mom and stepfather. I guess I would put my mom in the castrating bitch category, but at age fifteen I was only becoming aware of how much she really hated men. She hated Sarah too, chiefly because I loved her. So, I retreated to my room. It was my haven.

About an hour later, my older brother, who was fried on drugs all the time, came in and announced he had run over my cat. That news brought more tears, though I fought valiantly to throw them off. He just left the cat's body, limp and twisted, right there in the driveway. I was not having a good evening. I made this solemn oath that I would do something great for this planet if I could get off of it and go somewhere else. I was extremely dissatisfied with my life. I had been a rape victim by a man who claimed to be a friend of the family, but I had blotted that all out from memory. I had also already forgotten about my moon launch, but there was not much fanfare associated with it. It became kind of glossed over. Imagine having a secret like that one and being a kid and not being able to tell anyone.

School was the only fun and interesting thing in my life. I wanted to bring my girlfriend along when I got off the planet, but I didn't know that she would approve. Her parents were still married and her father had a good job at a bank, and her mom was well-respected because of the charity work she did. They were not scraping to get by like my family was. I was kind of a street urchin. At least that is what one school bus driver always called me. I resented being called that, because I had never thought of myself in that way. Her name was Mrs. Falls, but we finally made our peace and she left me alone after that. Because of some bizarre rule concerning the distance and commute, I could only catch the bus home, not in the morning to school. That meant I had to carry my bike on the bus, and though I had permission from the headmaster to do so, Mrs. Falls always complained. I finally threatened to have her fired and she shut up. Then we became friends of sorts.

When I projected that night—that very fateful night—like I always did when I slept, I went some place very special. It wasn't heaven. I've been there and it's boring. Beautiful, but boring. There's nothing to do but fish. I don't think you can drink in Heaven either, so what is the point in fishing. It is God's dark sense of humor. I don't get along with God. I never did really. I have also been outside the gates of Hell, but never inside during this life. Or maybe just briefly. If that was Hell I was stuffed in at a much later age, it is hard to breathe in Hell.

But the place I projected to was an ice planet. It was all ice and it was full of beautiful, cascading mountains of ice and flowing rivers of ice and cool sweet breezes. The inhabitants weren't Eskimos or anything like that. They were large red creatures with three heads and long tongues. That was my first introduction to the Goddesses, and things did not go my way at all. In fact, one of them sucked everything right out of my insides: my stomach, the entire contents of my abdomen, my lungs and heart, everything. I was in great pain when I woke up, and that had never happened before. I think I had traveled to the forbidden zone.

I would always do this isometric maneuver to get out of bed. I would put one hand in the other with my elbows bent and flip my body weight and roll out of bed. When I tried that morning, I fell right back on the bed. That had never happened to me before either. I learned isometrics in gym class. I loved P.E. and language training and my voice lessons were always good. I didn't dance or play an instrument. I wish I had learned how. So, even though I was hurting all over, I wanted to go to school. So, I did. I made my breakfast and used the last of the milk, and I made a mental note to get more after school. There was a grocery store near our house, and I always had a little cash because I mowed yards.

My house was too close to the school for me to be on the bus route going to school, not that that made any sense to me, so I had to ride my bike most mornings. It was raining this day, and on his days off, if he could get out of bed, my brother, who had a small foreign import car, would drive me to school, but this was a work day for him and he had left the house already. He worked in a bakery and got to work at five am. So I would have to ride in the rain, and I would be soaked by the time I got there, not to mention the extra time it took to put on my slicker and then take it off and stuff it in my locker. I would probably be late and the Dean of Boys hated me.

My teachers all loved me. I was smart and aggressive about learning new things. I especially loved Biology, math and Chemistry class, all of which were honors classes. The Dean of Boys told me comparatively I had the toughest curriculum of anyone in the school this year. And I was determined to make it into the honor society, which I did. The Dean of Boys was not usually friendly to me. I spoke my mind a lot and I guess things got back to him. His son was in our class and he was a lousy athlete and some of the boys made fun of him, but I never did. His family was poor like ours, and while the other students never really made a big deal of their parents' success, I always felt a little envious when hearing described to me trips to Spain and Switzerland and Mardi Gras and such.

My Spanish teacher was the coolest lady. I was in love with her too. She also told me she thought I was a saint. That particular comment came years after the funny little Japanese man on his bike said what he said to me. I helped her with a relationship problem she was having with a Navy Officer, and from what I knew of my dad's letters and Navy life it wasn't that hard to give her good advice. My advice spurred the comment that she thought I was someone very special. I have nothing against saints—I am just not a religious person. My dad was certainly no saint. He was a double agent I found out later. I am still not exactly sure what that means. He still wrote to me fairly often, and the stamps would come in from all over the world, and I treasured those letters, but I have never seen him since that night he left, except in Japan. Aside from that one instance when he went out for a pack of cigarettes, it has been eleven years so far.

My Spanish teacher quit her job after I left for college the next year, I heard, and I never saw her again either. I read and spoke Spanish at the college level when I was a junior in high school. I had taken two years of Latin before that. I took four years of Spanish, but never picked up a book in college. We read Caesar's *Gallic Wars* in Latin the second year and *Don Quixote* in Spanish the third year. All Gaul is divided into three parts: Beaujolais, Bordeaux and Champagne. I added that last bit. Caesar was a great warrior and statesman. They don't make them like him anymore.

Chapter Two

There came a point in my life during college that I realized just about everyone I knew had prayed to Satan. He's a punk, a real punk. He is funny some times, but this became my planet because it was offered to me by God. I had saved it; it was mine, but I abdicated. God, I think, was disgusted and walked away, which he has a habit of doing, and that left Satan in charge. About half the earth's population was Satanic by the time I was pushing fifty. I learned this again in 2049. The dates may seem mixed up, because they are basically meaningless, and I'll explain that at some other time in this narrative.

Satan likes to keep everyone down, not just blacks—everyone. I'm thinking of killing him, but I probably won't. I am going home and I may well just leave it at that. Besides, Satan and I go back a long way. Religion is all bullshit, I determined. I had been a rather devout Christian in later life, but not after a certain age. Religion is just a code of chores, and I don't like being told what to do. No one is really in charge of this rock, because no one wants it. Earth is the armpit of the universe. I think Satan is looking for his own way off, and maybe my family will help him, and maybe they won't, but it is not really up to me so much. I come from an illustrious family of time travelers. We are the most powerful family in the universe. I didn't know any of this for certain until I was almost fifty, but I suspected.

The visitors to earth, who are some of the most fabulous looking earthlings you will find, don't want to take charge of earth usually. They want to exploit the earth for their own gain. Money made in third world solar systems can be used elsewhere, if you know how. And the pickings are easy and lucrative on earth for aliens. It is a very simple matter to add a few zeroes to the left side of the decimal point.

I, on the other hand, am interested in living my life and taking care of people I love and myself, and I really could care less what else happens here. I know I finally get to go home. My real family has found me and I am out of here in a heartbeat or, as Keb Mo says, "on the note of a slide guitar." There are so many people on earth that are not from earth, I don't even know where to begin to tell you the half of it. You can bet if they have money and a nice family and beautiful children and a good career they are space aliens. There is a good chance as well they are not even aware of the fact. I wonder sometimes if that was true for Sarah and her family.

If they sit all day and enjoy coffee and espresso, they are not local boys and girls. At Starbucks all over my city, I refer to these guys as the men without jobs, but, of course, they are engaged in certain black market practices and internet schemes and spam, so they really do have jobs. They are mostly just Shitheads anyway. Shitheads are those I call that have prayed to Satan or been tricked into praying to Satan.

I don't think any actor or musician worth his or her salt is from this planet. That is one reason the competition is so rigorous. That rule doesn't stand for Congressman. They are mostly just ordinary Shitheads, which is actually the name of an invading race or species as well or, however, I should refer to them—I don't know—a race I could not destroy entirely. But they have become so intermixed with the Shitheads who are Satan worshippers, or at least Satanic, that they can now all go by the same name. Fighting the invasion force was the second miracle I pulled off and it was accomplished in the year 2049, so maybe I do qualify for sainthood. I might know in a few hundred years.

They are called by me Shitheads. I claim the first usage of that term to mean what I have said it means. They eat shit and are made of shit and give off a shitty odor like a pheromone. Oh sure, if you cut one they bleed, but their molecular structure is based on shit, not DNA. I suppose it is not detectable though by ordinary analysis. Anywhere you smell raw sewage, which is everywhere nowadays, there is a major Shithead nearby. If you tell one of their women she is pretty, she gives off her shit smell. Shithead women wear it like cologne. I prefer the Goddesses, but a nice young Shithead woman is a good break from the routine.

Shitheads are not the only problem. They also are not all bad. There are traits and characteristics to commend Shitheads. Their women are lovely to look at, their men are handsome, but kind of like a prize bull would be considered handsome, and a Shithead man is about as smart as one too. They remind me of Jethro Bodine. My Shithead mother always said her family reminded her of the cast on the Beverly Hillbillies. Satan is the King of the Shitheads on earth that are local boys and girls and by that I mean from earth. As I have said there are about three billion of them. I fought the invasion of Shitheads from outside the solar system, possibly outside the quadrant, and I mostly won, and lived to tell the story, but their sheer numbers were massive and I was injured and had to shut down. I was activated just for that reason. Somehow the CIA discovered it was I who would help them. My father had passed away, so I don't know if he had a hand in the government's affairs anymore or not.

But plenty of Shitheads slipped through my grasp. The entire universe was made of shit at one time, I gathered. I have no direct proof, but I suppose that to have been true. So earth has Shitheads everywhere now, and especially in the Southeastern part of the United States. The Shitheads love hot weather, and the Goddesses from the ice planets love cold weather, so they are mostly from Northern climes. Chicago, New York, places such as these.

Chapter Three

I was walking along the planet earth one billion years in the future, which was quite a puzzlement to me, seeing as how I knew the year was also 2049. That was the year the Shitheads hit the fan. And I figured out why 2028, speaking from my perspective as a fifteen year old boy, who was actually born in the '70s and reborn in the '90s, is the next truly important year in earth's history. Not that there are many people that know about what I did in 2049, especially outside the CIA. It seemed I had done the same thing in 2008. Confused? Me too.

I was watching 4D television in a McDonald's, when I discovered a potentially tragic future event. It must not have occurred though, because I was on planet earth one billion years in the future. The year 2028 is important because that is the year we can determine within the next seven years if a huge asteroid is going to impact the planet's surface or not. Anyway, I was next outside the McDonald's and nothing had changed on earth in one billion years, except television reception had improved dramatically. It was freakish, like some sort of parallel existence for the planet. Or I was simultaneously in two universes, the one where my consciousness lie and the other a parallel one for the events of earth as they had happened for billions of years. Maybe that is the key to time travel, being in two universes at once.

I had been traveling by car all over the southeastern United States, and I must have slipped into a worm hole. They are more common than people think, and I believe not just at the end of black holes. I can't substantiate that comment though. I am no physicist, believe you me. I saw people in cars shooting it out with invisible death rays, but the same people in the same cars kept parading through the drive-thru. Nothing seemed to be getting accomplished, and I was interested in watching the final battle on earth, but this could not have been it. Mexico had invaded and was winning the battle.

There were Shitheads that were local boys and girls, and I guess some of the Goddesses were in town. I might have been in Shreveport or Tallahassee. There were observers there as well. They were invisible as clearly as I could tell. I was meant to watch, and Jim Carrey was there and some other dusty looking man who looked like he had been on the time warp road quite a while. He needed a shower badly. I watched him depart through a bus stop. It reminded me of Dr. Who and his telephone booths. The dusty gentleman asked me if I cared to join him, but I could not be sure I was from his family. It might have been a trick. I was not sure if my family alone was the first group of authentic time travelers, and I did not want to go and mix things up anymore in case this man was not part of my family.

The Shitheads had begun a slow process of being completely dumbed down by Satan. Very few escape his grasp because of this. He and God are actually in cahoots, so any which way a local boy or girl turns he or she is screwed. And Christ really is dead, and if he did rise from the dead, which I don't dispute might have happened, he took the first bus out of town, and I seriously doubt he's ever coming back. So, the Christians just wait and wait, but then patience is a virtue. I sure as Hell am not coming back. I hate this planet. I hate everything about it except money and women. I hate God for what he did to me. And Satan is just a big nuisance sometimes. The easiest way to get rid of God and Satan is to ignore them completely, kind of like going cold turkey with alcohol or cigarettes, which is a process many have to repeat over and over to get it right.

Satan is a little gentler with me, after all the time I have been in Hell. My family has found me, and the members of my family will rip him a new tail if he keeps screwing with me too much. He knows it and he is imprisoned here as much as anyone, and my family can get him somewhere better, so he has an incentive to leave me alone, and more and more frequently he does. I don't hate him; I just don't care about him any longer. Satan is destroyed by indifference. And God could be dead for all I care. He's a punk too. But I love my family, and I am headed back to the ranch to be with them. I am the stray lamb, and when they sent out the search party for me 150 billion years ago, someone had the bright idea to check Hell and earth, and they located me. Yippee. No more backwards ass rock. I am going somewhere special, because I have seen it all, and soon again I get to live it all. And the two women I created for myself are going to share in the fun with me. We will be able to go anywhere and do anything we want. Those were God's final words to me before my family stuffed him inside my CD player in my car. "Go anywhere and do anything." Now to get even with me he scratches all my CDs.

There's no more Forbidden Zone in the universe. That was where all the ice planets were that were chocked full of Goddesses. God tricked me into visiting a planet in the forbidden zone, and that is when one of the Goddesses ate my insides. That's why I say he's a punk and a liar. I will most likely never forgive God for what he has done to me. 2008, and not 2049, may have been the actual year of his death. Zero, zero is the sign of the alpha and the omega, and while it did not all begin with the alpha, the omega spells the end of the alpha, so God may really be dead. Or he has just walked away again, and for an incredibly long time this time.

And if he is alive he will suffer at the hands of my real family, or his fate is already carved in stone. He tricked me into believing I was Jesus Christ when I was ten, and I went around telling everyone, so he had to send me into the Forbidden Zone, he told me. Apparently, I have been struggling to free myself from my fate for the last 150 billion years, and 2049 was my next chance and I pulled it off this time. Yippee. That conversation may have been a moment of truth between us, and that is when I asked my married acquaintance if she wanted to screw, because I knew it would piss God off. He has stayed out of my life since. I did not want to sleep with her though she is tall and lean and sexy, because she's married, and she said some other time. I accomplished my actual goal, which was to get God off my back.

Satan has better odds of surviving since he fed me all those years I was in Hell. I was bound and gagged too. I don't know the entire account, and what I was told may have been a lie, but if it was true, my family might show him some leniency for taking a little care of me at least. I don't know and I don't care. I would hope everyone has a good life on this rock, which means to me turning away from all religion and any expression of it. I know everyone's beliefs run deep, but religion is the most cockamamie bullshit there is. Then maybe the super powers that be will stop screwing with everyone. I am not everyone. I am no one, and no one escapes judgment. It states that in the Bible. But most people that believe in religion are not going to turn away from it—it is such a crutch—that will not happen, so I'll just quietly fade into the dusk. And I'll climb aboard the ship my family has sent. It is in the clouds somewhere. I don't have much time left anyway. At least not on this planet. Yippee. I can happily die and go somewhere else.

I've tried to kill myself twice, but I screwed it up each time. The second time I lay in a coma for three days. They wouldn't confirm that at the hospital, but I could tell by the way the nurse said, "so, you're awake," as if I had been unconscious the entire time previously I had been there. I wonder where I went during that time. Maybe I ironed out some details with my family.

The first time I tried, I slept for twenty-four hours. It was actually kind of peaceful. I laid out all my important papers, took several vials of pills, and turned on the Grateful Dead and went to sleep. My idiot wife awakened me and poured Epicac down my throat she claimed, which was probably true, because I was about to inherit a large chunk of money. If I had died, she would have gotten nothing, because it would have all gone to my sister and brother. Both times I have tried I used pills. My ex-wife wound up with nothing anyway, because I divorced her. She was not a good person in my humble opinion. She then remarried to a much older man with lots of money. Like my mom used to say about my sister: she would either make a million dollars or spend her life in prison—I felt this about my ex-wife. She was a beautiful Swedish girl with big tits and a mean disposition when she did not get her way, and she wielded a whip expertly. "Me and a friend sort of drifted along into S and M," as the song goes.

I have always had this theory of marriage and relationships that warm weather denizens should be with other warm weather denizens, and the same truth holds for those from cold weather climates. Opposites attract, but not forever, and too much friction spoils the broth. Resentment is the real destructor of a relationship. It is the little things that build up and kill a relationship. The key question I have found to answer in any relationship is: am I better off with or without the person? That sums it all up, but you have to be completely honest with yourself to answer it, and most people cannot do that. So another year or decade passes, the couple takes separate bedrooms and vacations, eventually leading to separate lives. And one or both of the members of a couple become more lost in their own affairs and further away from an answer. Then one day someone, the man or the woman, goes out for a pack of cigarettes and never returns. I feel like Carrie Bradshaw.

When you boil it all down, relationships of any kind don't really work very well for most people. But then most people are not loners like me. I guess they do work for some, but there are a lot of lonely, desperate losers out there. We love our boss, we hate our boss, we love our pets, we hate our children, we love our mistresses, we hate our wives—it all seems so confusing and byzantine to me. I write and I am lonely every second of my day, no matter who I am surrounded by, and my greatest relationship is with my computer and I hate my computer. Everyone I love, I hate just as much, if not more. That seems normal to me though. I like the birds on the wire. They are at a comfortable distance and they chirp so prettily and they don't beg for food unless they are hungry. In which case, I feed them.

Chapter Four

So, I don't know why this happened. I was ten years old and I did not remember until I was fifteen and then forgot about it again until I was nearly forty. I have no explanation. I was raped. He was a friend of the family. Got to watch those friends of the family. They are a lot like funny uncles. That night was my introduction to rufies. I am guessing that was it. Even though I was ten, I led my life like a man, and this lovelorn gentleman, head over his own high heels in love with me, sick, perverted, twisted man that he was, invited me up to his apartment for a drink. I thought nothing of it. I was a street urchin, after all.

I am writing now from my perspective as a fifteen year old boy, even though as I write this part I am pushing fifty. I thought I was done with my little moon landing, but no, later in my life the Pope decrees to be a Saint you have to pull off a second miracle. I wonder what miracles the Pope did. Sainthood status still did not matter to me; I led my life as I saw fit. It would, however, be nice to be remembered that way. I am not going to Heaven though. I wonder how many miracles the lesser saints performed and if they are even considered saints anymore. I thought I was Saint Drogo for a while, but he was kind of creepy. He spent the last thirty years of his life living between a hole in two walls. And he would only take the Eucharist for his supper. Other lesser saints would do creepy things too. They would do goofy things like pull their heads off and reattach them or float and moan like ghosts. Those particular behaviors do not appear very saintly to me.

So, this guy invites me up to his meager apartment for a drink. I go, and one sip of the drink, my knees start to wobble and the room starts to spin. I think at first the drink is really strong, but then I realize that I am being drugged. I make a dash for the door, but he's faster and slams it shut with me still trapped in his apartment. He then escorts me or carries me to his sofa and the next thing I remember is five years later. And when I remember it, it comes back full force with a vengeance. I see my limp, drugged up little body on the couch, my shorts pulled down to my knees, and my butt up in the air with a pillow underneath me. What an ignominious position. His fate will be an ignominious one. I could not see the man's face. I still have not determined who it was. But I know it was someone near to my earth family.

I remember the drive home the next day. My ass was in excruciating pain. It was trash day. The metal and plastic cans lined the road. He pulled up before my house a little, and said, "If you tell anyone about this, I will do worse to your sister." I believed him, but I still told my brother. My brother acted like he did not understand. It was our mother's favorite trick: play dumb and maybe the predator will go away or stop being a nuisance. So, as I am getting out of the man's convertible, I run to a garbage can belonging to one of my neighbors, and dump the contents of the can into his car and smash his windshield with it. He got out and chased me, but I hopped a fence or two and lost him and made it back home.

Some home I grew up in. It was a home for the criminally insane. No one even asked me where I had been all night. At age ten no one bothered to ask me why I had been out all night, or possibly no one noticed or cared. When I walked into my house I told my brother, who was getting high with a bunch of people that so and so had raped me. There was always some kind of hippie sit-in going on in our house. My mom and step dad were out boozing it up. Maybe my brother was so stoned he really did not understand. Or maybe the fix was in. I don't know if I pulled off my little moon job before or after I was raped, but I think it was the same year.

I still am unsure why my older brother died. I am living his life. He went to Princeton; I went to Harvard. He died at age nineteen; I had my first psychosis then. What was fated to be his life, and it was going to be God awful, was handed down to me. I have a hand me down life. I lived most of it, I think, before my true family found me. My true family found me in the year 2008. I was fifteen and pushing fifty, but I was born in the seventies. I can't be sure this is right, but I think so. It was 2049 when I actually performed my second miracle. And 2008.

The life of my older brother that died would have been handed down to my next brother, the chronic dope smoker, but my mother had made everyone in the family sign in blood an oath to Satan that they would do his bidding. My mother probably had in mind destroying her ex-husband, which she did an effective job of through the court system. So, she errantly destroyed his children in the process, thinking he would care, but he didn't. He was too busy playing spy and espionage games. No one, or very few people I should say, had an idea of whether or not he was a traitor. I heard both sides of the coin, and I don't really know whom to believe.

Satan was having none of it. Whatever it was that my mother bargained for, my eldest brother's life fell to me, because I refused to sign the blood pact. I don't know what age I was, but I was young, and I had no recall of this either until I was pushing fifty. I simply thought it was wrong to do so.

Satan is a putz. Putz in English means penis. I think the word is Yiddish. I describe earthlings that are not Satanic as putzes. Satan is not really a putz. The putzes have it hard. The cards are stacked against them. I had a lot of Jewish friends growing up because of the elite private high school I went to. I don't know any of them now, but one of my closest friends in high school was the attending physician at my second suicide party. He must have done a good job, and since they got me to the hospital, it was his job to save me, and he did. So, I have to express a word or two of gratitude. I wanted to die, but he didn't want me to, and he succeeded where I failed. So hats off to him. Yippee. If I weren't so worried about everything, I would enjoy my last few years, but I can't very well. I have plenty of money. This is not the first book I have written. Between my insane mother and father I wound up an emotional cripple. I am pushing fifty again.

Chapter Five

I have forgiven my family—they were all Shitheads. One of us had to take the high road and I released that anger and took that road straight out of town. They merely did Satan's bidding, and as they were in quite deep, past their elbows; they had no choice. My mother got hundreds of souls wrapped up in his crap. She was a very powerful Shithead, and I used to think she was a Goddess, another form of planetary invader, and that she had these powers other than what the Shitheads did, but I found out I was mistaken. She was just a Shithead and a local girl, I think. The Goddesses are much more powerful, and they don't hate men as much as my mother did.

And my mother had my brother and sister convinced that they were aliens and very powerful, but they could not do anything. It was all make believe on their parts; it was an illusion they swallowed hook, line and sinker. They had no power at all. This is my perspective as I push fifty. This is after my second miracle, so if anyone figures it out, I will be Saint Chris in a hundred years or so. I'm pushing fifty a little harder now, and yes, my Shithead mother is still alive. She's eighty-eight and today is her birthday. She's as nasty as she ever was. Some Shitheads don't die quite as easily. But like I said, I released my anger. She did what she had to, to survive. She is also my mom, so I am duty bound to give her some honor.

I hate Shitheads and I can kill them with a thought. They know it too, most of them, so they leave me alone now, so that makes me fairly happy, but not ecstatic, because I am surrounded by them. I am sitting at a coffee shop as I write this, and some foreign gentlemen, the ones I call the men without jobs, one of them just gave off his shit smell. There it was again. They smell disgusting, but these are little Shitheads. They probably think they are powerful, but they don't come anywhere near to smelling like raw sewage. The really powerful Shitheads smell like sewage and can actually stink up a city block.

I don't have anything more to do with my family. I am not a Shithead. I never was. Satan calls me, "my liege." He has to, but sometimes he forgets on purpose, but he is outranked by me and my true family. I have the Shithead frequency now though, so I can hear everything they think. A true Shithead communicates telepathically some of the time. There are more powerful Shitheads than Satan too. He is a local boy. They exist everywhere in the universe, or used to. I destroyed a lot of them. They thinned their numbers considerably too, because the smart ones knew I could and would destroy the stupider ones that serve no earthly purpose. They run their little black markets and their Internet schemes, and the slightly smarter ones run Ponzi schemes, but it really is meaningless earth bullshit. But it takes up their time, so they leave me alone. I am happy for that too. That is why the men without jobs have plenty of money. They're scammers and low level Mafia.

Like I say the Shitheads are not all bad. God hates them now too. He saw the error of his ways, and we made up as buddies, I think, and now he is going to help me instead of work against me. He has to, or it is straight back into Hell, and it will be my family that puts him there this time, not me. It was really they who put him there to begin with. My real family, not my earth family of Shitheads. And when they stick God in Hell again, if the members of my family have to, it won't be as comfortable as the CD player Hell in my car. There are far worse places to be stuck in this universe. God and I have tentatively agreed since our dispute healed that we would go deep sea fishing together. I'll bring my two, the women I created, because that is all I want, and they won't let me have any other women, or at least Rebecca, the dominant one, won't, and God is going to bring a dozen of his loveliest women. God's a player, but he knows how to have fun.

Sometimes his programming gets in the way, because God is artificial intelligence, but often it does not. He likes money and good looking women, so we at least have some things in common. I am really not very interested in playing with him, so we'll see about the deep sea fishing expedition. It could be a trap. I really want to become acquainted with my two, and go some places and be able to remain a while. It does not suit me that I always have to bail out and wake up just as the party is getting started. And I have plenty of virtual cash to be used in other galaxies. Billions, trillions, I don't know what it amounts to by now.

Chapter Six

There is one thing I detest about Shithead men, and that is how they treat their women. What I should expect from a Shithead male, I don't know, but it is frequently, and by that I mean more and more, that I see a particularly nasty occurrence of events that a Shithead male has done to a woman, usually a young woman. And often this woman is a member of his own family. Shitheads do not always begat Shitheads, but most often they do and their kids become Shitheads often in a slow process. The thing I have noticed is that through the use of force fields the Shithead male very often traps an unsuspecting woman in his car.

And Shithead men love to drive, and I will say this: they are excellent drivers. The Shitheads drive the virtual highway too. It was an experiment of my father's he let on once in a letter, and the Shitheads took it over. They drive on the wrong side of the road as compared with the typical motorist of the United States, and while that is not unusual other places, it is unlawful here. They don't stop for red lights either. Everything on the home planets of most Shitheads is reversed. So, if you see a company with the entrance door on the opposite of the typical side, which is the right side in America, there is a good chance it is a Shithead company. Entire industries are run by Shitheads, so they give the Goddesses a run for their money, but always come up short. The Goddesses are like the Borg from that science fiction show and they all think with one collective brain. Their brain power is unmatched here on earth. So the Shitheads push a little and the Goddesses shove back. My father must have been a Shithead, or for most of his life, but not the last few years or so. Shithead males are not much into their families.

The Shitheads drive cars powered by solar fuel. You see a lot of them out driving around when the weather is bad just to soak up what they can of the sun's rays. And they drive with their lights on when it is a sunny day. It recharges their batteries. Otherwise, their cars have problems. Any light will do, and since there was just a huge emission of gamma rays in the universe last week due to a large star collapsing, the Shitheads here on earth should have plenty of power to go on for quite some time.

Just the traffic lights and street lamps alone are enough energy to power most Shithead vehicles. The Goddesses drive around like soccer moms in SUVs and Jeep Loredos, and those types of similar vehicles and I don't know their source of power. I would be curious to find out, but I fought my invasion by the Shitheads and I defeated the Goddesses in the process, and I hope like Hell there are no other miracles in store for me. That was my second miracle, fighting an invasion again. I guess I cleaned up things nicely this time, but I didn't finish, but I don't have anything left, so it will have to do. I am not re-enlisting. The putzes can't drive worth shit and their cars are just regular old sacks of metal and cheap ones at that. Shithead and Goddess vehicles are rocket-powered. My Honda was a rocket ship. I never knew this till I was activated in 2008 and 2049.

I was discussing the trapped young women. I see these girls motioning to me, begging me with their eyes, and I see this often, but it is just a glimpse I catch, and I understand that they need my help to be set free. I did it for a few girls I knew that needed a rescue, but I can't really do it anymore, and I have no idea where any of these girls come from. The force fields shelter the girls from the sight of others, except I guess Shithead males and me, but it is really none of my business. Shithead males love to drive around with these girls trapped in their cars, and show them off to their buddies. They let their buddies rape them too.

I performed my second miracle and I am out of here on the note of a slide guitar. Like Keb Mo and me. Let the clean-up crew handle the rest. They are called Sweepers, and are something akin to mercenaries. They are mentioned in the Bible too. They can destroy the planet or leave it alone; I don't care. I'm not coming back. Jim Carrey and I will spend a vacation together, after we both get off this rock, and probably after the one day fishing expedition I go on with God. No tricks, God. Play nice. My two will be there with me, or I am not going. And it can only be for one day. And that is the time period as passed on earth—twenty-four hours. And I need some time to meet and greet my true family first. God, this is your only chance at redemption—so don't screw it up!

As for the Shitheads and their use of force fields: it never phased me. I would walk right through their most powerful setting much to my chagrin. It would hurt a little, and it is one reason I am in constant pain now, and they laugh because of it, and they can also get through their own force fields. They can lock up more than cars with them—universities, neighborhoods, even an entire major metropolis, I heard. And shit has no real solid basis, so it doesn't hurt them to pass through a force field. The ones that aren't local boys are not carbon or DNA based. They appear to be flesh and bone but they are not. The local ones can't spot the other out of town Shitheads either, but for me it is easy, because they are so much smarter than regular local Shitheads. I live in Florida, so the local Shitheads are really stupid. The out-of-towners usually don't give off a detectable odor either.

Shithead women are often a thing of beauty. They will do almost anything in bed, they are gorgeous, but they are also cunning. They don't usually have much in the way of education like the Goddesses who hold advanced degrees usually, but they have some sort of training and do well in the workforce. One of the big problems with Shithead females is they are into drugs so often. They were given horrible addictions when they took their earthly bodies. The Shitheads came here in the latter half of the twentieth century and were trapped here, and the Goddesses came shortly after, and me, I have been here for centuries, millennia perhaps. Only I could defeat the Shitheads and the Goddesses and in the process I earn my wings so to speak because of what I did. Earth really belongs to the putzes. And I gave it back to its rightful owners, but they are already losing it again.

Chapter Seven

I had two wives before. Both my exes live in Texas. Yippee. I did not have two wives at the same time. I am not a Mormon. Haha! That's all they get remembered for. I had a crazy friend once that every time he saw Mormons peddling down the sidewalk, he would scream out of the car, "Mormons." I am not even certain he was aware he did this.

My first wife was a Shithead of the local variety, and the second one was a blonde, beautiful, sexy Goddess. She was fun. For a while. It lasted three years between us and she moved on to greener pastures. She wanted more money, more money. Most of my cash is virtual, so I can't touch it, because I forgot how to. I did the best I could to provide for my second wife, but those Hollywood looks take a big chunk of change.

The Goddesses are not terribly faithful. I knew a lot of them in college. They love the pretty boys and are not shy about it. Some are very promiscuous. The Shitheads went straight to work on my second wife as soon as she got here. They convinced her she was a Shithead, but, in fact, they were wrong, because she had her own planets. No Shithead has his or her own planets. Everything belongs to the Imperial Wizard, who is this rather gay looking guy that sucks all the shit out of a Shithead's body and leaves them with nothing if they don't obey him. He tried to do it with me, but I killed him. I assume another one stepped up and took his place. He was dressed in this crimson ceremonial garb with a big black collar, and I killed him or he would have messed me up. But he wouldn't have been able to kill me, because I am not a Shithead.

So, my second wife had her own planets. There were seven of them I think, in addition to her home planet, which was a goodish-sized star. I destroyed her planets, and ripped her home planet last. I can be kind of nasty that way when I want to be. She kind of raked me over the coals, so I got even. Her earthly form was destroyed too, but she managed somehow to be trapped in some hideous form that she hated. I met up with her in a hospital a year or two after she divorced me. We were both in-patients. I ordered the nurse to give her a lethal injection, which the nurse did. My wife was in a lot of pain, and now she is free and probably reformed into something else. I know she is a squirrel. I heard her voice in my head for the last several years, so I then turned her into a squirrel. Now she frolics around my yard. I live on a corner lot with a lot of big old trees. There are plenty of nuts. I don't talk her as much as I used to. I am preoccupied with finding a life again. It's tough.

I kind of regret getting divorced from her, but I probably was not going to be able to keep her. She acted like a Shithead often, because the local boys had convinced her that was what she was. She was stepping out of the marriage more and more every day anyway. She was fun though, and she possessed the brightest smile, and that long blond hair and those legs that went on way past five o'clock. I could not really hold a grudge against her for too long. She is a Goddess. They are special creatures.

I was into sadism and masochism with both my ex-wives. I realize, of course, it was the time I was raped that prevented me from really having much chance of a healthy sex life, whatever that is. I was raped as a younger child too, before the age of ten. It was by another so-called friend of the family. Even so, I did have a quote, unquote normal "sex life" for a number of years, whatever it was. But she was fun. My second wife, fleeting, but fun. I didn't really have the money for a trophy wife at the time, so I was stripped of my crown.

My first wife I utterly despised. She was a local, ordinary Shithead without anything to commend her but big tits and a good sense for paying the bills and budgeting. That's something. I'll give her that. She could turn a penny into a quarter, but not a dollar bill. It was kind of a marvel. And the sex was good for a number of years. That's a fond recollection I'll give her too. But she sought to take advantage every which way she could, and I was not having it, so we parted company and she moved away. Tex-ass. She was all about the money too. The problem was by the time I had any, we hated each other. So, I decided not to share and went out one day for a pack of cigarettes. I never returned. She sold the house. The city had built a freeway through the front yard. I didn't care. I was loaded and just waiting to be plucked by the next gal.

That day I went to the ice palace and had my insides eaten was a rough day at school. I got there late like I knew I would and I was a soaked to the skin. I ran into the back of a parked car too, because my brakes on my bicycle were wet from the rain and wouldn't function properly. I screwed up my front tire. First period was Calculus, and my teacher was already drunk. He was a fun drunk, but then if someone pushed too far, or acted up the least bit, which it was usually me that did, he would erupt in the most venomous tirade, which was also a lot of fun to hear. The veins on his nose would double in size. Some of us had a running bet which day he would keel over from a heart attack, as he was easily in his seventies and that was ancient to us, a bunch of teenagers. He used to give us a quiz every morning first thing, and I had missed it, so I slipped in quietly while he lectured about limits under the plane. It was all the Calculus he understood, and we had been hearing about limits for a couple of months now. I wanted to get to the sexy stuff, but apparently it had to wait until next semester, after he was done with his refresher course.

My next class was American History with a young hip professor. He had a Ph.D from Chapel Hill, an excellent southern school, and he was witty and fun. He knew a lot of humorous stories about the presidents, and others in government, like the guy who wrapped himself up in the flag while he held a loaded shotgun and blew his brains out. It seemed funny at the time. American History was an advanced class as well. And then the day progressed fairly well from there, and Spanish was after lunch. I always had lunch with a buddy of mine on the lawn. Ironically, he was the one who saved my life after my second suicide attempt. It pays to know people and keep friends: something that has been impossible for me. They all take the fast rail out of my life when something goes wrong. He had become a doctor and he was the attending physician when they wheeled me into the emergency room.

Spanish class went well. I could always show off my talents with language in there, because no one ever bothered to learn their vocabulary words, except me and a few other students. My teacher always tried to conduct the class purely in Spanish, but it never flew. She was a great beauty and I loved her. It was more than the typical school boy crush. It was all unrequited though. Unrequited love and a love lost too soon are so painful. I can't bear anymore.

Most of the pain in my gut went away by physical education, which was always the last period of the day. We had flag football, and I was on the defensive line. I loved rushing the quarterback. It was a great high, and I was good at it, so my team mates always let me play the line, even though I was smaller than most of the boys. I would shoot across the line so quickly the offensive line could not block me. And I was no meaty linebacker type. I was a year younger than everyone in my grade except one girl, and my mother had me start school early primarily so she did not have to watch me at home anymore. She needed a break from kids.

I am pushing fifty again. Yippee. I have had four major psychoses, and I am here to say that if you have not had a major psychosis, you know not of what I speak. My take on psychoses is that the individual who is experiencing the psychosis is in two worlds at the same time. Or possibly one just leaks over into another. But he or she freaks out, and cannot behave appropriately in either world. This past psychosis of mine, 2049 the year was, and 2008, I saw things, and let me tell you, if you make it that far in your disease, which calling madness a disease is bullshit, then hats off to you, because you are going to have your mind completely blown.

Let the psychiatrists smoke that piece of crack. The ones younger than forty are idiots, and the ones older than forty are insane. My father hypnotized me and used me as shield for a job he pulled in Moscow at my age of nine, and how insane is that to do to someone, anyone, let alone a kid. I am here to say I am one of the meanest, toughest men in the universe and it is because my entire life span of one hundred and fifty billions years has been torture. And I have no recall, or very little, of how torturous my previous existences were on this planet, but I am sure they were no cakewalk either. Of course, I don't expect I spent all 150 billion years on earth, unless the earth is a lot older than we think.

And now I hate people, especially Shitheads. I made my peace with the Goddesses, even though they sought to kill me too. When I die and leave this planet, and I either die violently or all alone, I will go to debriefing and then take up the handles of my new life. It will be paradise compared to every stinking lousy moment on earth. This is one fucked up, messed up planet and I don't care the least piece of shit about it anymore. Putzes, I gave you a fighting chance. You'll probably lose and that's probably how it is supposed to be, but I resign. Hop on your rockets and inhabit Mars. Good luck with that plan. You'll need it.

Chapter Eight

I am of late noticing more and more giants. I think they are a jovial bunch at least. But there seem to be more and more women in excess height of five foot nine or ten. They're not Amazons either. The Amazons all died out years ago, except Xena. And at the same time I am noticing more and more men in stature of greater than six four or five. I am six feet one inches, so it is an almost imperceptible difference right now, but I think men and women are growing longer and leaner. It would appear just the opposite is happening, with everyone getting so fat, but the change I am indicating is occurring if ever so slowly. The giants are another race of invader and they are intermingling with earthlings, and they seem bent toward helping the planet. And they are not Shitheads, most of the ones now—the giants—are young are just barely out of their teens.

I know the NBA and the NFL and MLB have been full of these guys for decades now, but they are not true giants, I think, or most of them are not. The true giants are younger than Shaq. I met him or his clone once. If Shaq is a giant he is a very friendly one, as the giants all appear to be. I notice them in coffee shops, and around town, at malls, driving in large vehicles, eating big sandwiches, and wearing those plus-sized shoes. The shoes alone are a marvel. I see them on billboards, where everyone looks like a giant, but the actual giants look so much fuller of life when depicted this way. The giants are smarter than the local Shitheads too. I think somehow or another, they are here to help the planet. Or they may be cashing in on an easy buck. Perhaps earth is a paid internship.

Other than the plant people, I haven't really identified any other invaders. The plant people are certainly not human. They love their topiary and stay rather well disguised, so there's not much point in discussing them, because I don't know much about them. They have an evil bent, so I leave them alone. I was locked down in one of their Hells once. It was scary, but really more interesting, as I have always had a fondness for topiary. Seeing a topiary of Christ on the cross is a bit much though. But the fact remains that now nothing and no one on earth is who or what they appear to be. Remember the days when you had to be careful who you had a fist fight with, because he might be some martial artist type or a ninja. Well, those days have continued and gotten much worse, at least in terms of not knowing whom you are going up against. And God help you, if it is a putz. He'll shoot your ass. It is his only defense.

Everyone now is from somewhere else, and one has no idea what that other person knows, especially in the way of self-defense. The attacker might just be a pest who gets its wings ripped off. That is the world of earth now. And the poor putzes have no idea. They'll shoot anyone on sight now. And bullets are just a setback to some of these invaders. A Shithead will just reform and he will be meaner and nastier after he does. I feel badly for the putzes, because many of them are a boisterous, rowdy lot, who will go up against anyone, and have their eyes gouged out by doing so. I don't know about Army strong. I was never in the real military. I passed the officer's test for the Air Force, but that particular branch of the armed services wanted to offer me a missile silo position. Can you imagine Chris Devin with a missile in his hand. A nuclear missile. Or just the launch codes would be enough. It is designed to take two officers, but I am sure there is a way around it. Luckily, I will never have to make that decision. I turned down the Air Force's generous offer.

This is a rough period in earth history. Some of the nastiest aliens are imprisoned on this rock. Earth may really be a lockdown, a penitentiary, a penal colony. Earth is one of the nastiest Hells in the universe. Penal Colony Earth. A friend of mine said once we are slaves to money, slaves to our jobs, and slaves to family. I excommunicated the family part. And I don't work or have too much money that I can really use here. The notion of earth being a penal colony I find intriguing. Penal Colony Earth for mature audiences only. It would make a good video game. Escape with the loot and the women and the space vehicle and get out of town. Maybe the character can be based on Snake Plissken. Or maybe the Rock for the hipper audiences. I like the Rock. He is sort of a brother of mine like Jim Carrey.

Chapter Nine

I just met a friend and his wife for coffee. It was a chance meeting. He and I had been rather close. It was at my favorite coffee shop, which is closing because the company is falling on tough economic times, and I will lose just about everyone I chat with face to face. Luckily there are Romanian women willing to chat long hours on the computer. And they are beautiful and fun, but back to my friend. He's a local Shithead, but a smart one. He tried to shoot me and the gun backfired and blew his right hand off. It was through a window. I never went outside until later and when I did there was no blood, but it rained overnight and he could have been standing in the grass. There was no hole in the window, but the gun had backfired.

He taught my first wife how to poison people. He convinced me my second wife would make a good wife, which she really fell short in a number of categories. I loved her though. I had loved them both. My second wife cheated too much on me, and could not cover it up sufficiently, so I got hurt and became angry. Rather than putting up with my bitching, she filed for divorce. My first wife backfired too, as she is now in prison for poisoning her fourth husband.

I was given the opportunity to get even with everyone who had done me an injustice. Only it wasn't real in the sense it was not in my present reality. I was left one or right one or up one or down one, perhaps even a few. That is how the universe functions and all the parallel universes, or simply sometimes they are known as alternate realities. It is a huge grid that glows green with all the power that flows through it. I would think it would glow blue, but maybe there's so much power it leaped over the blue and went to a greener green. You can travel left or right, up or down, or up and left and down and right, and any combination. So, in my alternate reality, which is where my major consciousness was not accustomed to, I got even with everyone who had served me a cold dish of revenge. This friend was one of the major players. The rest of his life will not go well, because the realities at some point spill over into each other. His wife was always very sweet to me, and since she is a Goddess, I left her alone. The Goddesses and the Shitheads intermingle too.

I did not really seek all this revenge on the unsuspecting hearts of others, but I was pushed along in a crueler, more hostile reality, and there was nothing I could do about it, but go along. Revenge seems to be a universal concept. That much figures. And I really did not care that I hurt these individuals who had done such a number on me in my major reality. I became a little bit of an animal. My whole life has been one massive set-up. Illegitimi non caborundum. "Don't let the bastards get you down." That is bastardized Latin. The phrase does not really exist in Latin, but someone came up with it and pawned it off as actual Latin, but I know better.

Anyway, I saw this man and he had no obvious clue of what had happened and he had a right hand still attached, and it was not prosthetic. So, alternate reality it was. I traveled through several parallel universes, possibly at the same time. Worm holes can do strange things. That must have been how I did it when I was a kid. I remember one of the parallel universes it was always night out, no sunshine. I had this very cool laughing bird I called it when I created it. I would say, "Where's my laughing bird?" and it would laugh like a mocking bird, but sort of half-human, and I could tell it was much larger than a mocking bird.

I was sorry to see him go, when my reality sobered up again, but that was a kind of harsh animal universe with all these odd lizards too. They were too big to be Geckos, and they looked absolutely prehistoric and fierce, and I had never seen a lizard move that fast. They surrounded my every movement outdoors. And sometimes they were not there at all, so I knew I had awakened in another universe. It could have been I was in the Hell of one of the plant people's variety: odd plants, weird animal species seem to go together, like birds that don't flinch when you throw a cup of coffee at them.

I didn't like it there much and it never rained. I would bump and grind and come to a stop in various parallel universes and it would be daylight for a period or it would rain, and I would know I was where the major part of my consciousness was more or less, but I felt depleted, drained. Too much hopping around universes. It really wasn't for me. I just wanted to find my own, tried and true reality back on earth and finish my sentence and go home. And I did, after the year 2049 or thereabouts. In addition to being the year 2008, it was also the year 2015. And now, lo and behold, I have Sainthood coming too. I performed my second miracle, and even though that Pope is dead, it has not been upped to three miracles, so as soon as they discover what I did, I will be anointed, as a saint.

When I was a kid it mattered not, but now that I am pushing fifty again, it matters more to me. Why not go out as a saint? Who gets to do that? Freaks, that's who, but no one said the path to salvation and sainthood was an easy one. Thank God (I'm being sarcastic) I don't have to go to Heaven. I would probably have to farm the land, or some God awful job like that. Naturally, I would refuse and get booted from Heaven with no place to go. Imagine being homeless after being in Heaven.

It was another fine day in paradise. I was sitting on a curb outside where my rocket Honda was being repaired. It was just a regular car when I bought it, or so I thought. It really came into its own in 2049, which was also 2008, and was probably the best rocket ship I could have gotten for the money. Apparently, I don't just project. Sometimes I need a ship. It could get me home on terra firma hundreds or thousands of miles and light years on an empty tank and it never broke down.

Some Shithead had disconnected the battery cable, and while I was handy enough to figure that one out, it screwed up the CD player in my car. I had to enter a code, and I had no idea where the code could be found. It was probably one of God's people, thinking he was turning off the force field in my car's CD player. It was a crude attempt at setting him free, because I don't use Shithead technology much, and the attempt failed because God is still in there. God's people were the first inventors of Shithead technology, and the Shitheads don't even know that. Anyway God stays there until my family says he can come out. And, of course, he is already out, because that event has occurred, but to me I don't know when or where that happens, but it has, and it is happening, and it will happen. And this might go on endlessly. Yippee.

Anyway, I distract myself even. I was sitting on this curb when I got my first glance of the known universe including all the parallel universes. I was seeing it in my mind, and I could tell there were a lot of people in my head at that time. It was kind of like they were looking through my eyes but it was really through the eyes of my mind. That seems like a rare treat. To be able to do that I mean, not necessarily my mind's eyes, but maybe that is a rare treat too. It's like they know what is coming, but then if it was my family of time travelers, they would know what is coming next, because it had already happened. They would at least know what was coming at some point in the future, which is meaningless to them as it has already occurred to them. I get the feeling a lot of them are scientists. I respect scientists, but not doctors. Give me a nurse any day over a doctor. Doctors are well enough educated to be sure they are not idiots, but the joke is on them. They are idiots.

I still like my buddy who pulled me out of my second suicide attempt and the successive coma I was in. He has earned my respect for all eternity, which ends fairly soon, I think. Eternity that is. That is why the concept is for all time, but time ends eventually too, but not as soon. So then the concept becomes what lies beyond time. I respect my friend for what lies beyond time. That's a lot of respect. He was a good friend in high school too. We were best buds and I'll never forget that. We'll meet again and I'll do him a solid.

Since my family travels in the fifth dimension, the fourth being Einstein's invention and better put, his explanation, of time, which opened up the doors to an understanding of time travel on earth, my family may actually already know what is farther out than time. I have calculated it is thought, the fifth dimension, but I don't know how to do anything with that just yet. I have to have a major shift of consciousness and that doesn't occur until I get off this rock.

I do slide as well. But sliding is a vehicle of time manipulation that I do. I think lots of people can slide and do, but maybe don't even know they are doing it. I slid three times in 2049 just to survive. I had to get out of my accustomed time zone and go back or forward a day or two. Sliding has little to do with thought, which is the fun stuff now. My true family grew very bored with time travel, but now, because of me, the members of my family have a new toy: traveling at the speed of thought. I created the fifth dimension. It was an unusually long and complex equation that I set my real big brothers and my robots to, and they solved it, so it is real. My true family of time travelers may be the only ones who know how to manipulate the equation. Imagine having a patent on the fifth dimension.

I suppose I will have to get up to snuff with a lot of history. History is a good measure for understanding the future. And when it all occurs everywhere and all over the place at the exact same moment, it should be a lot of fun to ramble around in this huge known universe and all its parallel universes. It is like turning the pages of a book. You flip them forward and go forward, and backward and go backwards. Just don't get too immersed in the book, or you might not make it back to where your major stream of consciousness is. And that is a very good thing for a time, but you still have to put the kettle on for tea and fix dinner.

So, I was sitting on this curb, and it was hot. I am bound and determined to continue this part of my narrative. I had shoes on fortunately, because the asphalt was roasting me. The sunlight kept splashing up in my face as a reflection from the road. It was blinding.

I see this green grid in my mind. It takes up all my mind's sight. It's huge, but I see it from quite some distance so it is like I see a miniature of the known universe. Diamonds are like that. I see all the grid lines, and of course, it is glowing green, which Kryptonite was green, but I don't think that has anything to do with this. Of course, my dad might have been Jor El, and then my brother or I am Superman, but that seems unlikely to me. I'm not able to jump tall buildings in a single bound, but I bet I could fall off of one handily enough. Yippee.

So, this grid is a marvel of technology which far surpasses any artificial intelligence we have here or other places. It is pulsing, vibrating and growing. That part was almost imperceptible because I saw it as a miniature. But I do see how the grid is wired, so I can get around obstacles and free myself and avoid entanglements, but that's not a theory I want to test. I want my family to get me the Hell off this planet and that will take a ship. I did my time, I paid my debt to society and I think I was kidnapped to begin with, so it is time for me to leave soon. Good riddance. Rat's ass. I had to throw in the gratuitous curse word, but it really is how much I care. It is an accurate measurement. This planet blows.

Chapter Ten

The thing about a psychosis is that it is all real. Since nothing is real on earth, a psychosis is as real as nothing gets. It all occurs in the mind and usually the psychotic individual, in this case me a number of times, rarely has any visual proof that the incidents are real. Most schizophrenics or otherwise psychotic individuals don't see things. They don't hallucinate visually. That was one of the major distractions of the movie *A Beautiful Mind* about the Nobel Prize winning economist, John Nash. The real man I was informed did not have visual hallucinations. That part was Hollywood.

The brilliant economist is schizophrenic and I am sure he had his fill of auditory hallucinations, but I don't think he ever saw one thing that was not truly there. Or more likely since none of it is there, we all see things that are not truly there, unless we are blind. And then who knows except a blind person. It doesn't really matter at any rate, because if Mr. Nash had seen something that was not there, it would have really been there anyway. Nothing is there, so everything is there too. That's not hard to understand. It is simply left or right one or two parallel universes. And if you get caught in a jam, there is plenty of help in any universe, or at least for me there was.

The CIA did a lot more to help me than harm me. And what I did for the organization, I can't be specific on, because I don't really know what I did. There were lots of voices vying for attention from me, and I saw all manner of things—some of which were brutal and shocking—like the plant people's Hell and all the incumbent torture I was served in getting there. 2049 was a rough year. I was pushing fifty.

The biggest realization of my pushing fifty was that this body does not have that many more miles to go. And that is a very good thing. One famous author said, she was going to fight old age like Hell, kicking and screaming, and roller skating or something like that into her coffin. I am much less aggressive than that, and as a result middle age has crept up on me and blindsided me, and it's not pretty. The funny thing is no one dies until the exact correct moment in his or her life. That doesn't mean go and jump out of a plane without a parachute, because I think maiming oneself or just shattering bones might happen to be a random event.

I now have very bad arthritis and I am in constant pain, and it seems fairly random of an occurrence to me. I don't know when it started, why it started, or how it started, and I don't know anything to do about it except munch some pills for breakfast and dinner.

Plenty of people want to believe that everything has a reason, and I was one of them, until 2049. Now, I think some things are causal, but there are plenty of good things and bad things, occurring on a daily basis, that are not. Sometimes the randomness is the cause and sometimes things were just meant to be a certain way. That means that certain things have always been a certain way, are that way, and will always be that way. And it could mean the exact opposite is true too. I don't really care that much though. There's no monkeying with the past, because it is always that way, and if one does successfully throw in a monkey wrench, and outcomes change, it is still the past and still that way somewhere. And where the wrench lands is just another parallel universe. This is how we approach infinity. As infinity expands, so does everything else with it. An infinity is not merely an endless progression; it is an infinite endless progression. That may seem redundant, but it is not.

I wonder how people that know what they are talking about view this. They probably have a very different viewpoint, not that I care. They are all aliens, but I wonder if they know that, or they simply must wait until their 2049, which has already occurred, and their consciousness expands so greatly. Or for some maybe it happens before then. Maybe there is a random process that is switching people on left and right. That was actually a pun: left and right, because of the way one travels through the universe. Who is to say these individuals switching on are switching on where their major consciousness is. They could be switched on over and up or down and out, etc., etc. And where their major consciousness is, they might not realize they are switched on somewhere else.

Chapter Eleven

It turns out my father was a major Shithead too, as I have stated. I had always suspected. In one of his last letters to me before he died, he told me he had hypnotized me, placed a number of post hypnotic triggers in my brain, and that he was the one who drove me crazy in college to cover up something he had done. He went on to explain the KGB were looking for me because he pulled a job in Russia when he was there. I have maintained all along that I have never been to Russia, but in case I have and have merely had it erased from my memory, I was acting as some kind of unwitting scapegoat for my father. The Shithead. I did nothing wrong and broke no laws, if I was even in Russia, which I doubt.

He erased my memory so I would not react as though I had ever been to Russia because I believed I had not. I still believe this, but it is coming more finely tuned that I may have been there with him and his second wife, who also was a Shithead, and he pinned everything he did on me. He was fifty and at the top of his game. To top things off, he might not have been working with the approval of the United States government, but instead acting like some rogue cowboy spy. He faked a heart attack soon after and then retired. I have felt like he used my sister for something too, but not nearly as involved as what he used me for. She was already a Shithead, and I am not and have never been, so he may have left Maggie in Satan's care.

I wrote him back and asked him to clarify himself and a few points, but he conveniently died before he wrote back. I did see him at the crematorium. Someone there, probably a Shithead, had painted some bright purple smile on his face. I'll never in all my years forget that expression. It mocked me from the oven he was hoisted into. It said, "I know a lot more of what I did to you than you'll ever discover in this life buddy boy." My father, the brilliant psychiatrist, the CIA muckity-muck, the Captain in the United States Navy, was a cruel, immature man who was afraid of everything and everyone in his life. When his number was up he died alone with no one to console him or comfort him, except a prostitute. Rest in Peace. You're in God's care now. Haha! Yippee.

That is the end of that part of the saga. I had limited parental supervision, and limited contact with my family on earth, my friends have all deserted me—I am alone—except for my real family. And I don't know how long it has been since I have seen any of them. Certainly in 2008 and 2049 they were all around me. They will protect me. I have faith. In them, not any religious icons. We were around during the first big bang, or at least maybe subsequent ones afterward, because my theory is there have been multiple big bangs. They are real, my family, and I wish to be reunited. I don't know for sure if I was sent on a mission, or if I was kidnapped. I know I am young, but I am very damaged in this life.

In my next life, I will have my two, the warrior queen Rebecca and the beautiful submissive Chloe, and I have my rightful big brothers, one up and two up, and I have a family that loves me and wants me home after one hundred and fifty billion years of searching for me. How heart wrenching and joyful it will be to see my real parents after all this time. It has even been a very long time for them. The parades, the parties, the music. The food. And all my family will be there if they can be. Jim Carrey, the Rock, Steve Carrel. Gary Coleman. I am bringing a lot of people from the planet earth too. That is a note to my family, so get ready. The more the merrier. It is my triumphant return and I am hiring the Rolling Stones to play at the party, and socialize and mingle, and rest and stay, if the band members would like. I am joking about that part.

Chapter Twelve

My second miracle. This is what earned me Sainthood, not that I feel very saintly. I destroyed a few invading species. It seems I was trapped in Hell again, but I knew I was not trapped permanently. I was on a mission. Kate Moss and Michelle Pfeiffer were being held hostage in a house in the Miami area, not far from South Beach. I did this one all alone, and I never saw the pair of women. I had been challenged to put my money where my mouth was and rescue these two fine ladies. Who could resist? I had been told Kate Moss was dead, and she would actually be reborn as her former self in all her glory, if I saved her. I dearly loved Kate Moss. I met her at CBGB's in New York once. She invited me to join her at her table, but I declined because I was there with my girlfriend. I was told Kate died the next day, and she was dead when I heard her voice in 2008. I heard her voice from the grave.

I thought she and Michelle Pfeiffer would join me, if I was successful and saved them both, and we would live some sort of idyllic life on earth, the three of us together. I was led to believe as well that they were in actuality Rebecca and Chloe, my two, and could not get out of the house that held them prisoners, so it was up to me to rescue them. My two had done everything to protect me. My loyalty was assured.

The house was down a long cul-de-sac after a very circuitous path into the subdivision. I found the house right away. I pulled up in the driveway, and immediately my car got stuck on a brick embankment circling the drive. It was a small car and an even tighter squeeze into the driveway, but a voice told me I had to go behind the force field. The voice thought it was trapping me inside with the others, but I could walk or drive right through the force field. They hurt a bit, and these were strong force fields, but it was easy enough to get through them.

Luckily I always carried a crowbar in my trunk, but I had to free these women first. It turned out the crowbar was necessary for that as well, as I had to bend the frame of the door back on itself to allow enough room for the women to fly out. They were in some Goddess form I was not completely familiar with, so they could fly and were invisible, but I could hear their voices. I began to believe it had nothing to do with the ladies' earth counterparts, and I was actually one or two or more parallel universes over, left or right. And from that vantage I may have been two or three or more parallel universes up or down. It is impossible to say now. I have become almost completely deactivated. And I am in constant pain.

So, I set my favorite model and one of my favorite actresses free, but of course, it earns me no chips where my major consciousness lies, because none of us were on earth. But I did a good deed anyway, somewhere, so I felt very good about myself. It came time to free my car, which was a snap, and drive back home. I chipped away at the brick embankment and was free. As I pull out on the interstate to head back up North, the most amazing thing happens. I realize the timing was perfect, even if the event was horrible. It was timed so I could fight some more. I had been on the highway all day and night and had not slept in a few days as I recall. And then the worst fighting of all came my way.

It began to rain shit. Shit was coming down all over my car and all around me. It started oozing into my car through the air conditioning vents, through any crack it could find. My tires were barely gripping the road, and I was not going slowly. I had to figure something out fast. The stench was becoming unbearable. Luckily Kate Moss and Michelle Pfeiffer had flown off, so I knew they were safe, and I had completed my mission successfully. Now, I just had to make it home safely, which seemed questionable that I might do so. I truly thought this was my last adventure. I thought I was a goner for sure. It would take wits to get out of this one. So, I convinced the shit that was falling from the sky that it was actually ice, and it transformed into ice and died. Shit is nothing when it freezes. It was the worst ice storm in Florida's history, and this part I suppose won't hit the press until 2049. I heard no accounts on the news in 2008 of any major ice storms in south Florida.

But my car was really slipping and sliding because it was actual and authentic ice on the roadways. It was about four o'clock in the morning, so there was almost no traffic: just me and my rocket Honda on the roads. I zipped along icy streets about ninety miles per hour, and who knows how fast I was really going. The speedometer was just regular Honda issue. I could have been traveling thousands of miles per second.

It was the largest invasion force to date that I had ever seen. The tonnage of shit was huge. What slipped through as shit and remained shit would be good for the crops, I guessed. I couldn't be sure. I drove along I-95 North and left Florida behind me. I was safe after that, so I slowed down.

Epilogue

It must now be 2009 or 2050. My ability to fight anymore has been stripped. I am deactivated, and I am in constant pain. I am prey for the tiniest punk aliens that are out there on planet earth, but they all leave me alone now. That is something different. I used to be picked on in every public place I went. And sometimes the Shitheads would gang up on me.

There was a time when I was having lunch and two Shithead males jumped me at my table for no reason and I had to scuffle with them both right there in the restaurant. The manager of the joint screamed at me, as though he was going to call the cops on me, even though I had not started anything. I didn't even know who they were. Another time a crazy Shithead came after me at a bar. I knocked him out. Cold. And then I got out of there. Other times I have had to fight too, and I never started a thing. But now everyone leaves me alone. I guess you have to destroy a whole fucking army to get any respect from Shitheads.

And I am always alone now. I am a shell of a man. I am a spent cartridge. Everyone knows what I did, and they are curious who I am, but I just say I am not a Shithead and leave it at that. I don't inform anyone I am a time traveler anymore. It is too complicated, and they don't believe me anyway. I live alone now. My roommate moved out. My mom has passed, and the rest of my family does not come around anymore. I am still in touch with my one sister. I was broke and could not work, so I was forced to sell my house and move into an apartment. It's better that way. It is less stress and less to deal with, and I can play it on a lower key. None of my friends made it through with me. They all turned their backs on me, even after I was relatively sane again, which is no admission I was insane, because I wasn't. But then clearly I was.

I sit at coffee shops and read, and my greatest social affair now is flirting with the girls who serve me coffee. I fall into a chair because I can't bend or swivel my hips and I won't go under the knife again in this life, and though there is no reason for me to pray, I hope death finds me soon. I want to go home, to my real home, and now I seem more stuck than before. But it is simply not the right moment yet. I know I make it off this rock, and it is probably just in the nick of time that I do. And so it will be for a lot of us, because I have amassed an army on earth that is coming with me. Timing is everything, especially on this planet, which is all I seem to know for now.

My knuckles are all shattered, my gut is torn up, arthritis has crept up my spine, and every day my hips hurt. I am in with a new doctor. He's kind of a simpleton, but then I convinced him I could take care of myself, so he applies less and less pressure for me to follow his orders, which don't make any sense anyway. Medical care on this planet is almost a thing of the past. I am sure the government will outlaw it.

I still drive. I traded the rocket Honda in on a new one and I can see this new car has potential too. I go and buy groceries, out for coffee, and to get my hair cut. I can't work. I don't think I'll ever be able to again. So, I sit at home in my small one bedroom apartment and I listen to a lot of music. The tears have passed and I have regained a little more sense of who I am. I venture out on the Internet looking for friendly photos of women who will listen to my problems and hopefully make a decent recommendation or two. I watch the news and cook dinner. I take pills that help me sleep, and I flash back to last year much less than I did. The flashbacks were excruciatingly painful. I know what combat veterans go through. Trust me. I know.

I always fancied a military life in this life, but I was ill too soon, and could never join. There would have been complications. My father was tacitly disappointed when I turned down a commission with the United States Air Force. He thought by remaining quiet about it, he could goad me into it, but I never brought it up again in our letters. I was always one step ahead of him. Saving the planet twice would have to be my reward.

I am now on federal assistance. I live in HUD housing and use food stamps to pay for groceries. I get disability, but it isn't much. I am destitute. Satan, the supreme Shithead of earth, in all his efforts could not break me, but then he did not have to. Prison life on this rock was all it took. This is one great big cell, and you do your time and then go home, if you have one.

I know my family is here. I have a home. It may take months of deprogramming, but I will assimilate into a better lifestyle with my true family once again. And if this has all been a mission, some sort of planned endeavor, then I am probably done, and I will retire soon. It is not that I look forward to retirement, but I will have my two, and my true big brothers, and a royal family that loves me, of which I am a part. I am ready to go. Take me. Yippee.

A Trick of the Devil

A Novella

a sequel to *Don't Cross the Devil*

By

Cameron H. Chambers

Also by Cameron H. Chambers

The Stone Cabin

For the Love of a Madman

Confessions of an Internet Don Juan

Don't Cross the Devil

www.cameronhchambers.com

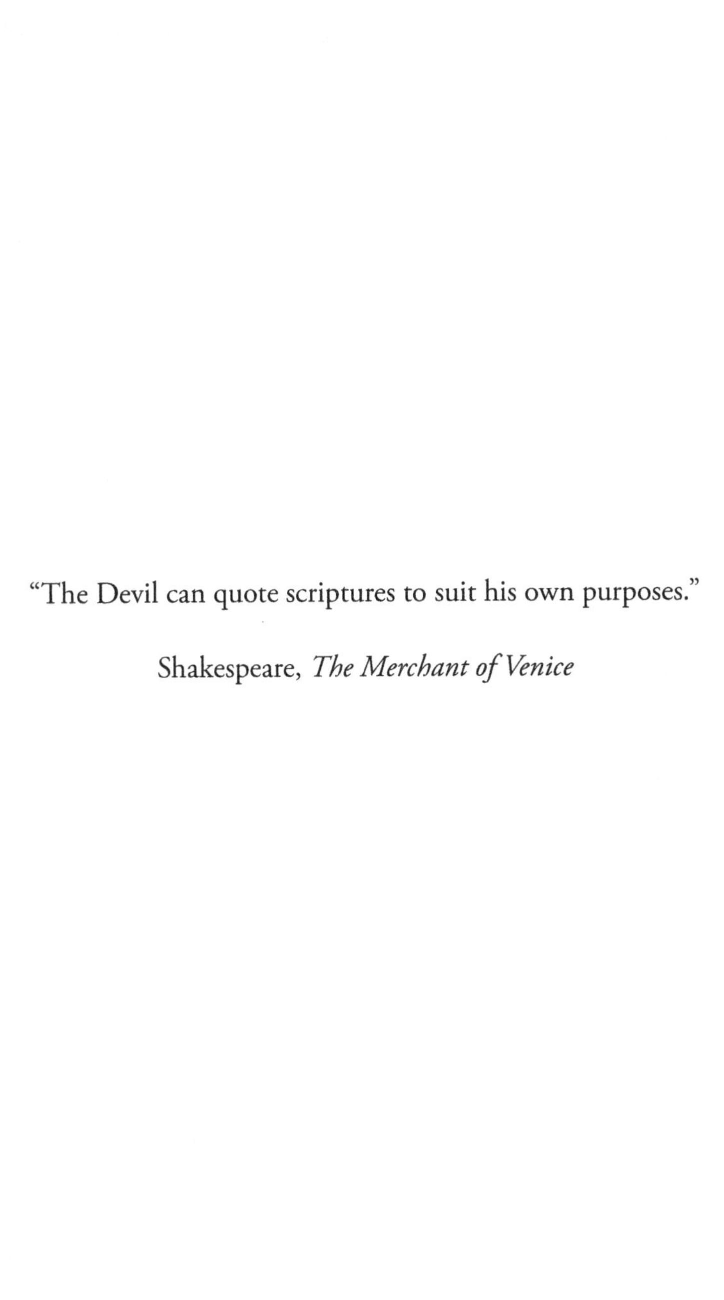

"The Devil can quote scriptures to suit his own purposes."

Shakespeare, *The Merchant of Venice*

Chapter One

The site was Jacksonville, Florida during a warm November. Silka and I were attending the Blue Man Group concert. That is where I met her. Where I met the other girl, or young lady, not Silka. Silka and I had been together almost a year by then. I'll call the other woman Jenn. I am not too clever with names. The real Jenn was actually a waitress at my favorite coffee shop. Silka and I decided to step outside onto the patio of the Veterans Arena in Jacksonville. The lights from the street lamps shone brightly. There was a church steeple and a green bridge visible from the patio.

We had driven up from Orlando and were driving back to our apartment in Orlando after the show. The show was kind of silly existential crap, with depressed nothings from the great existential writers broadcast on huge monitors, but the drummers, of whom I think there were seven, had the most amazing set of percussion instruments I had ever seen.

Silka and I now lived together. Her disabled brother Hinton lived with us too. He's educable mentally retarded and a sweet kid, but he doesn't speak much. We had gotten a three bedroom apartment recently in a nicer complex in Altamonte Springs, away from the CrackDonald's off U.S. 17 where our previous apartment was, so I could use one room as my studio, even though I had not painted in a while. I had gotten my insurance check for the paintings that were stolen from Chanel's gallery, and if there's one thing money will do for sure, it's take the edge off an artist. Somerset Maugham said success is the worst thing that can happen to a writer. It goes for painters too, I guess.

The three of us, Silka and Hinton and I, were talking about moving to Jacksonville. We did not like Orlando any more. The traffic was horrible. Jacksonville couldn't be any worse than Orlando. Jacksonville is a hicky, rednecky environment, but then God loves a working man. It would be Silka's third major city in Florida in about one year or a little more, after migrating here from Hiawatha, Kansas, and for me, Jacksonville represented a return to my roots. I spent some years growing up in Jacksonville, which was first named Cowford. The name still fits aptly enough. Jacksonville is right there nestled in the armpit of Florida. It smells, but then it clears the sinuses.

I am Chris Devin, the so-called son of Satan, but who I met that night in Jacksonville, Jenn, not the real Jenn, but the young woman I am calling Jenn, changed my life and my understanding of myself forever. And I do mean forever. I am not the son of Satan; it became clear to me. I am not a son of God, either. I predate them both and believe it or not, they are real entities. I, however, am a time traveler and an Immortal. People on earth think God is the creator of the universe, but he's largely sneered at around the universe. God is a machine, well, at least about ninety percent machinery. God is artificial intelligence. Before I destroyed him and then brought him back, I called him Brian. He's really not that bright either. He gets duped constantly.

I'll tell you how I know this; I'll relate the entire rest of the story—right up to the invasion of earth. This is part two of the story. There is a part that I went through before Silka arrived and after she was on the scene and she rescued me the first time. I saved her life once, and she returned the favor a few times. Silka is not a part of my true family. She's not a time traveler. And all my family, my true family, not the peons I was associated with on earth that call me their blood relative, of whom all that is left is a heroin-addicted sister and a sociopathic mom in an asylum, and those two made me to believe they were my gene pool, but they are not. My true family members are time travelers. My real family is comprised of all time travelers, and I have met several of them, and they are really outrageous and fun individuals. The most famous one on earth is the actor Jim Carrey. He must be an older brother of mine. There's a funny story about Jim Carrey and me smoking a virtual jay outside a McDonald's, but first things first.

We, my family, scamper around the universe doing whatever pleases us, which in most cases means observing matters and events, and I am sure our fair bit of tinkering with circumstances and situations. Star Trek's non-interference directive sounds like so much irrational blow. Interfering with global and inter-planetary disharmony is too much fun. And I am not too ashamed to say I was a Trekkie as a lad. The original version of Star Trek with Shatner and a Klingon for a first mate that really looks like a Klingon. But that's all made up crap. But some of it's true. I've astral projected to places like the ones mentioned in all those glorious made-up sci-fi movies and programs. My astral projections took place mostly in my youth, but I still go on occasion. One must be in good shape to travel.

There are apparently a great number of us in my true family, dozens, hundreds, thousands possibly, and where I fit in the hierarchy I do not know, but probably somewhere along the lines of where a child might fit. Earth might have been a rite of passage for me. If I could escape a penal colony, one where everyone's memory is erased each life, then maybe it is on to bigger and better things. I do not have all my answers yet, but a lot more in this my almost fiftieth year on earth in this life, than I have ever had before. I now know who and what I am; I don't know how I became so or where exactly I'm from, but I have more answers now than I did at any point previously in this life.

And asking who am I, the greatest existential question of all time, is a load of crap for most people to wrestle with. The answer in most cases is you're nobody, but there are those and many among us, who are someone, and I was either recently admitted to those ranks or had already been in the mix. I don't mean to brag, but I saved the earth, and I have a propensity toward bragging anyway. It could be genetic, but I don't know if that applies to me and my earth family or not. Genes and DNA are sort of a limiting equation. It is not a good thing being a braggart, I know, and it gets me into trouble more often than you might think, but that is just some Puritanical guff I grew up with. The assholes in the South think there is some code against bragging. I say if you did something, shout it off the rooftops and the guard towers.

More likely I crawled out of my crib and had wandered away and was tricked into becoming someone on earth, that is to say an earth bound someone, and this deck of cards played out for centuries and seemingly got worse and worse. My last life, which is to say this current life on earth—which is to say my last life on earth—I am schizoaffective, which means I suffer from schizophrenia and bi-polar disorder. I know it all now sounds like the tendencies of a fruitful and paranoid imagination, but I assure you my story is factual. It is at least based in fact. Some of it is true, I guess. I am not really certain how much anymore. All right, it's all true. Or none of it is true. Only the names and faces have been changed to protect from whoever might sue me.

When I had first met Silka, I was just recently activated, which is to say my sixth and possibly seventh sense had not been turned on prior or not in a great number of earth years in this my last life. I really had little clue what was going on, but my entire life I had been made aware that my father was a nasty alien, and he claimed he was Satan, and he constantly screwed with me. That might not have even been true that the man, or whatever type of alien he was in actuality, was even Satan. I've met Satan a few times and he seemed somewhat jovial, a likeable enough creature. I never joined up with him for anything, because I'm not from here, and maybe he is not either—I don't know and I don't care. Maybe he got stuck on this rock too. But the true Satan was always polite to me—he was vastly a gentleman, and a handsome entity. He worries about his looks. He has a reputation to uphold with the ladies.

And the one who claimed to be my father and my second father who claimed to be Satan were probably just a pair of wanna bes. Both were powerful and nasty, which is a deadly combination, but it landed my biological earth father in very hot water. And Satan too, if that was he. I think my true family fixed both their wagons. My father, the alien, might have been a Shithead; they are an invading and colonizing alien race, and there are huge numbers on earth. They are everywhere on earth. I find it a pity. I fought them and defeated their army, but many slipped through. In so doing, I also defeated the Goddesses, who are another invading race of alien creatures, only all females.

The deal was down so I would become the next owner of Hell, which would have meant I would have needed to call Hell home. I've been there. The landscaping is rather grim. Dead trees and craggy rocks and such like. That was the deal with the one who claimed to be my father, who also claimed to be Satan. But I never wanted that for myself. I'm not into torture and all that sadistic stuff. The deal involved the fake Satan, who had to kill me or incarcerate me in Hell or something like that. I am not privy to all the details. I was just an earthling as far as I could tell, prior to being fully activated, one who was sent messages from all over the universe, but I attributed most of that to my schizophrenia. Freud was the stupidest man that ever lived. Or maybe he was an alien. They obfuscate matters a lot. My true earth dad, not my fake father, but my true earth father who never claimed to be Satan, was a Freudian psychiatrist among other noteworthy accomplishments. He was mostly just a huge jerk though, but a very well trained doctor.

Silka is an earthling, which is kind of surprising because she is such a beautiful creature, she could be mistaken for one of the Goddesses easily enough. She did become switched on briefly, however. She is six feet one inches in heels and one hundred and thirty pounds soaking wet with long blonde straight hair, green eyes and a sweet can. And sharp as they come. The Goddesses were the rulers of the previous dimension of creation. I have known a lot of them, slept with a few, fallen in love with them once or twice. My earth mother was their previous queen. That reign of terror has passed. She is in her nineties and just now starting to die. My mother went insane in her later years and is locked up in a mental institution.

When I was activated, I ushered in a new dimension, even helped to create it. And I saw in my mind that I had separated the old dimension from the new dimension I am in the process of creating. A dimension, one dimension, constitutes the entire known universe at that time. Dimensions get pushed left and right and up and down, a kind of layering effect. The older previous dimension, that is to say the one I ripped away from the one I created, became a parallel universe. There are something like forty or forty-five parallel universes at present. The number of them has the capacity to be infinite, so creation has a long way ahead of it.

I was told I had done this on numerous occasions, which makes me think I am a part of some sort of ruling family, and we are possibly the inheritors of the earliest dimensions. Their work has been passed down to me, but I have been on earth, which is a really stupid and backwards rock, for so long that I have forgotten how many dimensions I go back.

And make no mistake about the Goddesses; they still have razor sharp teeth and tongues, even though I defeated them. And they are gorgeous, as I have said, bright, articulate, good mothers sometimes, but they hate men some of them, but there is still a lot to commend them. They play a good game still. It's a game of never say die and take every advantage they can, and why not? That's an earth game in some respects, but they are not earthlings.

The Goddesses go back four dimensions or three parallel universes at most. They can also travel in and out of these parallel dimensions, and this happenstance makes them appear to be time travelers, but they are not. I think they leave a fragment of their consciousness in the dimensions they were once in, but now that I separated this dimension, or the known universe at present, from the older dimensions, they can no longer use their old tricks to go back and forth in time, or what appeared to be such. So if there was trouble afoot in one dimension, they could back out and resettle in another locale and then come back when things settled down, but they are bound by this universe now. Their next leader, who was an offshoot from my mother, told me as much.

In their natural form they have three heads and will devour anything. You have to cut off their heads before one of their heads swallows you. It's a tricky matter. They suck out your insides with their long, pointed tongues. I've seen it done before. One of the Goddesses was in a tree in my front yard of my old house, and an alien creature with something like a light saber swooped down to the ground and then with great stealth popped up to the tree and separated the one Goddess from her three heads. It was fascinating. I was not on drugs. This really happened and I saw it, even though the alien who helped me was invisible. I can see invisibility. I never caught the victor's name, even though we spoke telepathically. He may have been the Anti-Christ. He had every reason to help me, if I am or was the Christ. With me out of the way and on the journey back home, he has solid control of earth.

Every planet has its own frequency, and I can communicate with virtually every alien on earth and around the universe. Some are so intelligent they don't bother with the likes of me with my little earth-sized brain. I can't even figure out how to go through a wall or fly or turn myself invisible. I get the help I need though.

And as for earthlings I love them with all their petty problems and almost complete lack of understanding, and there's a lot to love about them. Earthling women are supportive and kind and have a general attitude of being helpful. I have fallen in love with a couple of them, but that was probably back in high school. Until I met Silka. Silka and I are in love, I think. At any rate, I know I love her. I wonder if, when she becomes activated at some point, she leaves me.

In college, almost all the young women were Goddesses. The Goddesses function something like the Borg on that other Star Trek show. There are a few million or billion of them, and they all have one collective mind and can operate as one. That is indispensible while taking college exams. They communicate by what passes for telepathy on earth, but it is all just a radio frequency the entire race of Goddesses share. They sought, almost every one of them at my college, with unerring passion, to kill me, but they were unsuccessful. I have dodged attempts on my life for what seems decades now. From poisoned drinks to locking me out of a dorm in sub-zero temperatures in my underwear to all manner of unpleasant behaviors, they sought my death; otherwise, they would become relics and things of the past creation, which they already have for the most part. But I still love them. There are a million or so in the United States alone. What's not to love about a brilliant, beautiful woman, or in my case, women, as there was such a multitude at my college. Down South, where I am from, the Goddesses are not as plentiful. I went to a ritzy liberal arts college in Iowa.

That is where my earth dad, not the Satan look alike I refer to as my father, but my earth dad sought to drive me insane that first time. In college. He was successful. I had all the immunities to poison I could stand, but psychotropic medication and alcohol are not to be underestimated. He hooked me up with a nasty little colleague of his from medical school while I was away at college, and the two of them conspired to rearrange my brain chemistry. So, I flash back to those years a lot. It was the last time my life made any sense. I had two full blown psychoses in college. Honestly, I don't know if he was protecting me or not. He was a lousy dad. He went to his grave without explaining a thing to me about what he had done, other than the fact that he had hypnotized me. He was a wimp. He lived in denial like most wimps.

As I said, I thought I was an earthling, just with some unusual talents and curses, but my switch got tripped. I wonder if it all was fate and meeting Silka had anything to do with that. Fate is a kind of an earth-centric notion though. So is God and Christ and all the other religions. In fact, my father, the one who claimed to be Satan, said once he invented them all—he meant the world's religions. He may have—I can't say with any veracity who might have done it. Religion is mostly bunk. I have little remembrance of specific past lives, in spite of those silly past life regressions, except being a Samurai and a Mexican gunslinger. Good ones at that. The world's religions were intended as just another layer of deception for the non-alien dwellers of earth to fend through. The Bible says Satan's greatest advantage is convincing others he does not exist. I don't think so though. He's a nice guy . . . I mean the real Satan. But he is also a wimp.

But according to the universe, and God's place in it, God is kind of a regional player at best. The concept of God may exist on earth alone for that matter. He's real, but aliens around the universe stick out their tongues at him. He did not invent the cosmos. God is a liar and a fraud. That's for sure. The thought that he created the universe is laughable. He doesn't go back enough dimensions. He doesn't even go back as many as

I do, but possibly more than the Goddesses, because they call him father. He may have tricked them too, and convinced the Goddesses that he created them, but it is possible they go back further than God, because as they tell me, the Goddesses are always tripping up his programming. God has programming problems constantly. So maybe they tricked God into believing He was their father. His programming errors are an embarrassment too. I feel sorry for him.

There may have been a big bang, but the original one was a lot longer ago than anyone can remember. Even Time has no conception of how long ago the original big bang was, if that's what really occurred. Time can't remember accurately. I've seen Time, but he doesn't talk much. I spoke with him once. He's just an old white-haired man like everyone imagines that sits around a lot on a sort of lonely throne. God has no clue when the original big bang was, or even if there were multiple big bangs. I asked him. He hedged. He was attempting to lie, but I could tell he did not know. Trust me, this narrative is not in the most part about God, but he did play a significant role the last time my switch was tripped. It's probably obvious I am mad at him for the tricks he played on me. I am angry with Satan too. They will get theirs.

God had given away the planet earth originally, I believe. He then tricked a man, just a regular young man, Jesus, into rousing so much rabble that the Romans and the Jews executed him. God claimed Jesus was his son, but that's not exactly accurate. God must have lost earth in a poker game or something. God hated Jesus anyway, because he had offered the planet to him, and God wanted it back, so God created a martyr of his one and only supposed son, and this was the perfect way to put earth firmly back under God's control. The truth is God did not have a son. God is mostly a machine. They do not procreate in flesh and blood, and let's put to bed right now the myth that God is infallible. He did not have a son. Not Jesus or Mohammed or anyone. Not one I know of anyway.

Back to topics more interesting. Even though I considered myself a Christian when I also considered myself an earthling, most of whom—the Christians that is—I refer to as putzes, when I learned I am not from earth or of earth or God, I gave up all religious aspects of my personality. I digress again. Forgive me. I started out by telling about Jenn. She was this ginger-complected and ginger-haired girl about twenty-two or three years old, and an exotic beauty I could not take my eyes off. I only saw her the one time though. She had joined Silka and me on the patio on a predetermined lark, it appeared to me, to speak with me about my work, and she was so engaging and had a fabulous knowledge and understanding of my paintings, which intrigued me, of course. And then she told me I was going to be involved in a fight and I would be in constant pain from the time it began for the rest of my "stay," as she had put it.

"So, why do I get in this fight?" I asked.

"It is to save the earth and almost no one here will know what you did, until you start bragging about it, which you will, right, Chris?"

"That sounds like me," I said. "Then will they want to lock me up?"

"That dream will come true too, but not for very long. Just overnight." And then she communicated telepathically to me, *Silka will actually see that you get hospitalized again and that you receive proper medical treatment. She's a good girl for right now. I approve for the time being. But.* I could tell too that Silka had not heard our telepathic conversation. Jenn, or the woman I am calling Jenn, not the gal at the coffee shop, went on talking in an aloud conversational voice all the while communicating with me telepathically. Earth putzes, and let me reiterate, I love them, and Silka is my gal, and I adore her and love her, cannot figure out things through telepathy. They will receive the messages sometimes, but not really understand or know of the origin. And they quickly dismiss them as a conscience or a subliminal or subconscious response or their little man. They might even think they are their id or ego. Freud was amusing if nothing else. Earthlings never really made it far past Medieval times in terms of intellect and knowledge and understanding.

Are you like my mom or something? I asked. I was thinking back into Jenn's mind.

Something like that, Chris. And your father is here too, and he's not the one who you have been told is your father. And he's not your earth dad either. Do you believe me? Jenn asked.

Yes. It's bizarre enough what has been happening, it has to be true. So, I kill someone. "I don't want to do that," I said out loud. Jenn and Silka were talking about hand bags, and Jenn's college—she had just graduated in August from the University of Michigan with a degree in business—and the pair discussed Orlando and local employers in Jacksonville. At the time I remarked out loud that I didn't want to kill anyone, Silka shot me a look. It was an imploring one, as if to say, please don't listen to the voices now. I know you are schizophrenic, but not now, Chris.

I mixed things up a lot; I was a physical person and fisticuffs were nothing new to me, but I only fought in self-defense. I had a bad reputation in Orlando. I had gotten in a fight with a high school chum a couple of times, my old nemesis, Jude, and he smeared me all over town with anyone who would listen. I messed up his face a little and knocked loose a crown. And I know it is deplorable behavior for anyone over ten, and I am almost fifty, and that means I am not much better behaved than the apes that come after me, but at least I hate that part of me. I have a long draw on self-loathing attitudes, but I do create some popular paintings, and art that people seem to enjoy. I'm not all bad; I am, however, realistic about myself and honest with myself. Jude would have done much worse to me if I had let him. He was always a hot head.

Meanwhile, Jenn didn't skip a beat with me. *You kill an invading race, several invading races, and they are much more sophisticated and deadlier than you at present, and it's by the millions, perhaps billions of them. Maybe trillions. We don't care. This is your planet, even though you are coming home to be with us soon. You're our secret weapon down here,* Jenn said. *You will hear the phrase used. Secret weapon. Remember.*

Like I said, I had that unshakeable reputation of a fighter around Orlando, even though I was middle-aged. The mental illness and all. It scared people even though I am a kind hearted man. There was a true dichotomy of those who appreciated my gentler instincts and those that wanted to bash my head in. I had grown up scraping for money and jobs and women. Many young bucks wanted to take a swing at me, but they were mostly afraid, and I just didn't care for it, so I could get nasty and rude to them. I would often taunt them and all the while verbally embarrass them.

They are either Shitheads or plain ordinary white trash.

The Shitheads are an alien species, as I have said, made of shit. They eat shit and are hard to kill, but I figured out a number of ways. They are everywhere in the United States and throughout the world, I guess. I think it explains why so many people die in bombings and warfare, etc.

But in Orlando, some people were truly scared of me, though I was a gentle lamb; I am, however, an imposing man, almost six feet two inches, and two hundred and ten pounds with a large, muscular upper body and I possess great agility and deftness with several martial arts. That part of me, Jenn informed me, was about to be eclipsed as I was going to fight an inter-galactic invasion. The martial arts would work on some species and entities and creatures, while others would laugh at me. And I had to figure out how to defeat them.

Only a brief part of my fight would be hand to hand. My life would never be the same. Jenn also told me Silka would be the only one who would come to my aid that was not a true family member. Virtually everyone around me would be some sort of enemy combatant or potentially so.

Not only had I been activated, I had been called up, and Jenn said I would fight and that I would do so willingly, because this dying rock would die sooner without me. Earth apparently had been my home longer than I thought. And this almost dead rock belonged to me. As soon as I fully realized that, I left the earth in the form of an inheritance to the putzes. The Shitheads, I think, were the first to invade originally, even before the Goddesses who came around the early twentieth century. Fighting the next wave of invasion troops was the only chance earth had. Somehow I had to get all these aliens, whom I think were destined to become trapped on earth after they came here and attacked me . . . somehow I had to get them all to communicate with each other and work alongside each other and together; otherwise, this earth was doomed and all the inhabitants of it.

I was the only chance earth had. I was going to save earth and piss off millions of aliens in the process. There's no point in fighting unless you can really hurt someone, or help them for that matter, perhaps cripple their might, or redirect energy, or anger them terribly, but then I was basically a peaceful man, but apparently I was called to duty. A soldier's life does not belong to him or her. And I had always dreamed of soldiering in this life.

My earth putz dad had been a soldier, a US Navy Captain, and a spy and a clandestine high-up muckity-muck in the CIA. And to boot he was a psychiatrist, I have said, who spoke about a half dozen languages and tricked people by hypnotizing them so he could steal their money at poker. He was a terrible dad, but he was always doing something interesting, right up until he died. His forty year younger prostitute girlfriend was with him when he died. He died penniless and he had made millions. And then there was whom I had believed my father to be, the fake Satan. He died owing the IRS back taxes. And I had always been the cavalry coming over the hill for both of them, even the Satan wanna be, who was so nasty to me. But on occasion one or both of them bailed me out of a tough spot, but it was usually after they had put me in those circumstances to begin with. I thought they were my family. Even earth family can be wheedled into doing the right thing sometimes.

So Silka and I left the patio of Veterans Arena in Jacksonville and went in and somewhat enjoyed the second part of the show by the Blue Men Group. It was something to do on a Sunday night. I would never forget Jenn. The memory of her was burned into my retinas. I would never forget what she said either. I had finally met a true family member. So, my heroin-addicted younger sister, who probably was just some kind of earth putzy witch or a shape shifter, was just some stranger like she had always been. And my brother who died so long ago was probably not anyone related to me after all. And my other brother who died was just a warlock or some such. I found relief in these notions, but the creeping, invasive loneliness that came along with the realization was almost crippling. I was finally alone, what I had wanted, but not in this way. And all whom I had in this life was Silka and her brother Hinton. Silka and I drove back after the show to Orlando. She was not tired and was very animated actually.

"What are you going to do tomorrow, Chris?" Silka asked.

"I hadn't thought it about it yet. Probably fix breakfast for all of us, and coffee and get coffee for me, and take Hinton to his school, and maybe I can paint in the afternoon. I am thinking of trying to paint in the afternoons now."

"That might be good. Then you don't have to get up so early and go to bed so early. We could have evenings together a little more. Now that I have quit my second job, it would be nice if you could stay up later."

"Then, it's decided. The afternoon light is little glaring in my studio, but if I get a different type of blind for the window, it might filter better. I am the only painter I know of that actually likes to work by incandescent light. But my eyes are now not what they used to be, and that room has a western exposure, so it might be better to paint in the afternoons."

"It must be tough to paint. Everyone says how hard it is and how it drives artists mad in the end."

"Madder perhaps. You have to be kind of screw loose to paint to begin with," I said.

"How do you feel?" Silka asked.

"Pretty good. The show was dumb," I said.

"I thought so too. I thought you might like all that philosophic stuff."

"Not really. Philosophy is so personal. It's like a brand of toothbrush. One size fits all junk is kind of nonsense."

"Are you sorry we came?" Silka had suggested getting out to a show and seeing this one.

"No, not at all. That was the neatest set of drums I have ever seen. If we have a house ever, I would like to put those in the garage."

Silka laughed. The drum set was three stories high and there were easily over two hundred pieces.

"How do you think, Hinton is?" I asked.

"Oh, he's probably asleep by now. He watched television all night, I'm sure. He's fine or he would have called."

We drove the rest of the way to Orlando and chatted and held hands in the car, and it was nice to have my gal by my side. I had been turning in early lately, and I felt like Silka was missing something, but I just have been so exhausted. I decided to try and see what I could do to improve on that.

Chapter Two

I was in the small farming community of Grinnell, Iowa. The town of Grinnell was home to a rather prestigious college named aptly enough Grinnell College. Horace Greely, a journalist among many other things, in his immortal words "go west, young man" spoke them to Josiah B. Grinnell, a Congregationalist minister, and he and his troops made it as far west as Iowa. The college was established in 1846. I attended from 1978 to part of 1980 and then again in 1981 to 1982. I had two full blown psychoses during those years, which I always attributed to Reagan being elected president, went to lots of parties, and met some very special young women. My love for the Goddesses is authentic; it won't erase or rub off easily. I wear them in my heart. Their precious Borg-like minds are a thing of great wonder, and their dedication to work and fun and especially social causes is unparalleled. And at my college, they came in all shapes and sizes, and were beautiful, every last one of them. But I had a mission. I had to defeat them to make this a better world.

Of course, as I have said many of them sought to kill me, but not all of them fortunately, and there was still a lot of carousing and sex and drinking with the brilliant beauties, and until I went crazy, and then went crazy a second time, it was a hospitable enough environment, though nestled far away from civilization in the corn fields and the emerald rolling hills of Iowa and its ten foot snow drifts. The Goddesses always preferred a cooler clime; they come from an ice planet, and as I have said there are not as many down South. I recognized their intellect instantly and not one opinion fits all kind of mentality, even though they all thought with the same mother brain, my mother's brain as it turned out to be, and they recognized instantly the fire in my belly. They liked me. Or I was good in bed, or none of that mattered and it was just a small school, and everyone knew everyone else. They were fun and inventive, and after I defeated them years later, they still had their uses in many fields, as quite a number went into medicine, science, technological fields and education.

I don't want to mention specific Goddesses by name because many of them were murdered by the CIA. The CIA had to do it, because in the previous dimension, no one ever gave up, or if they did it was just a pretense. I turned the two most powerful Goddesses into birds, so they could at least survive, but I made them the same gender, and of course, that was female, so they could not procreate with each other. The CIA, which is my adopted family, and I am not sure if they adopted me or I adopted them, but the organization's members did a number on the Goddesses. So did the Shitheads. But the Shitheads don't possess the same intellect. They are mostly men and tough ones, but not cunning, more like bulls that gore you if they can. Shitheads are about as bright as bulls.

The CIA has a great number of very powerful aliens that work for and among them, and know of other aliens in other organizations, and one of the CIA's central goals is to protect the earth, the entire planet, not just US interests. That may not sound like the CIA most people know, but I assure you it is true. I was reluctant to join them at first, very reluctant, because they tortured me, but when we finally proved our usefulness to each other, I joined the family for a brief time. I am now retired. I saw a few of them here and there, but I have long since forgotten what those individuals looked like. I couldn't pick them out of a line-up, and the organization's members run the gamut; they are from every walk of life, many are married to each other, some are aliens, some are not, some are immigrants, and some are the people you would least expect to help you. But they will.

Even though by nature I am a braggart, I have to give the CIA most of the credit for saving the planet, if that is actually what winds up being the case. I think they are still implementing plans to follow through on some matters, and these matters are classified, so I have no clue about them. I never got a security rating; I guess there was no point. For that matter, I don't know if I was officially employed. I was promised the highest level of retirement benefits in case I live a long life in this last life of mine on earth, and I was promised fifteen million dollars, so maybe all I was, was a subcontractor or a mercenary. I am yet to see any money.

If I wanted to see into the War Room or the Oval Office or other places of interest I would just close my eyes and concentrate. I can't do it anymore, and that ability will never return I hope, and I only did it a couple of times, because everyone asked me not to. The War Room is just like what I had seen on television once. I think it was in that Mathew Broderick movie, the one in which he plays a deadly game of chess with a computer that is launching missiles.

My earth putz dad, brilliant as he was, was a double agent, and he set up America, and was actually considered a traitor for a time. He may still be considered such. I am not even sure my earth mother, whom I don't visit anymore in the sanitarium because she has not only gone insane, she has Alzheimer's and does not remember me, but I am not sure she ever knew her husband of many years was a double agent. He screwed his country, America, in the mid 60's. I was just a young child. And he had to abandon in a hurry a lucrative psychiatric practice in Jacksonville and flee to Japan. He took with him a new wife, fifteen years younger than he, a bundle of cash, and orders to do something in conjunction with the CIA, which, I believe was setting up the Yakuza to take a terrific fall. And this is what brought him back to a place of honor in the CIA. I'm guessing; I'm not certain.

The time was ripe for his going, as he had divorced my mother and murdered his eldest child, who was a freshman at Princeton. My earth putz dad enlisted in the US Navy as a Seaman, even though he was a doctor, and was the most quickly promoted person to Captain in the history of the US Navy, and may be still, and I always thought it was because he was so smart, but he also had important connections.

I was four when he fled for Japan. I didn't see him again until I was nineteen during my first psychosis. My schizophrenia it turns out was all induced by hypnotism. He had set me up to take the fall for a job he pulled against the KGB in Moscow. That may have been the job that saved his neck, but then he had the KGB sniffing after him. He had the spy stuff in his veins, and he died of old age. His veins were like ice water because he sure didn't have any blood in his body. The KGB were looking for him, and for me, so he drove me insane with pills that triggered hypnotic influences placed in me when I was very young, and that was when my schizophrenia developed. The bi-polar disorder came on me later from the stress of the induced schizophrenia. Remember, he was also a Freudian psychiatrist.

The KGB quit looking for me and left me alone. Madness is worse than death, so there was no point in killing me, but recently they started looking for me again and it culminated in a big fight in the year 2008.

2008 is when all this went down and it went down almost the entire year until August. I'll explain the significance of the year later on. At any rate, I whipped the KGB into shape, which means I destroyed about a third of their top ranking members, but really it was the CIA again that did this, and it was done to protect me. Many Russian women are Goddesses and employed by the KGB. If you have looked at the Russian women available on singles websites, it is not hard to believe they are Goddesses. The Russian Goddesses are rich and beautiful and bright, and they take advantage of American men in particular, because it is a good way to infiltrate the country and then work at overthrowing it from inside. The KGB is full of aliens too, and they mostly would not give up, and I was already a member of the CIA by then, or a subcontractor, so when the KGB attacked me, and they did unmercifully at first until I knocked off a very powerful Goddess, and the CIA just picked them off one by one. The KGB is not as well trained as the CIA.

My dad had forged flight documents that made it look like I was in Moscow in 1980, but I have never been to Russia. By the time I divorced Alison, my only wife, the KGB was hot on my trail again and they meant business. That was 2008. By then I had been on the pills my earth putz dad put me on for so long, there was no way to counter the side effects of the pills or the hypnotically-induced schizophrenia, nor was there any chance of getting off the pills. I was in my first psychosis in 1980 and in general felt miserable. I had dropped out of college, left my Goddess girlfriend behind in Iowa, because I was of no use to her, and I spent much of that year locked up in a psychiatric hospital.

So when I could, I went to live with my dad when I was nineteen, and within the year, he escorted me in his Porsche Carrera to a convenience store a mile from his home with all my worldly belongings and the ten bucks I had in my wallet, and told me never to come back. At that time I had a drug problem and I made the mistake of asking him for help. That was the last time I saw my earth putz dad. He was a lousy dad. He died when George W. Bush was elected president.

The Satan look-alike contest winner I saw rarely too. I saw him on his death bed because he needed me, so I showed up. He claimed he was the one who hypnotized me, but I figured out later that was a lie. He was what I guess is called a shape shifter and could change forms, so he looked like my earth dad, only about twenty years older than the last time I saw my putz dad. I suppose he could have been a clone, but I don't think so. Clones of humans are not usually very intelligent. I thought it was my earth dad I was going to see in Florida Hospital in Orlando, because he had informed me he was dying, and that he was leaving me an inheritance. I did not even know we lived in the same city. He had never given me anything before, but a difficult set of choices, and nearly impossible ones at that, and a greatly lessened will to live, so I thought if there was something for me in all this, I would at least check it out. I expected my heroin-addicted sister would fight me for what was left, but my dad or my father, whichever one he was, had already taken care of that contingency by specifically disinheriting her.

That was when I discovered, or shortly after, that I had two fathers, and they both were basically evil and disgusting. One was a man, and the other was an alien, who could shape shift. I pretty much despised them both, and it was sitting around talking with Silka that made me understand there were two creatures involved claiming to be my dad.

I remembered too what Jenn had said telepathically. *Secret Weapon.*

It was late the following month, December. I had had a good year financially and bought lots of toys for Hinton and me for Christmas. He loved playing Risk and Monopoly with me. We were getting on like brothers. My older brother had died of head wounds on Christmas day. Someone had cut his brake linings. We all understood our dad had done it. It was his way of saying don't talk too much or not at all. I was four, and I heard so many different versions of the story that I never really knew what to believe, but my CIA family informed me it was so. My other brother had a heart attack at a much later point in his life. My CIA family didn't lie to me that much, if ever. But everyone else did, and since a lot of what I was gathering as information came as voices, some filtered, some not, in my head, it was often hard to tell who was whom and who might be giving me the straight skinny.

"That's enough. I am done wrapping gifts," Silka said. "My parents never gave Hinton this much stuff. You're spoiling him. Remember he grew up on a farm. He labors for his keep, and I would have him do it again, but he can't drive in the city. Maybe he can find some kind of a job in Jacksonville. I learned a lot about responsibility from the hard, painstaking work on a farm," she continued.

"Do you miss your family at Christmas?" I asked. "This is two in a row without them."

"Yeah, we all went our separate ways when our parents died. The boys all took to the cities near Kansas with their girlfriends and got jobs, and I moved to Florida."

"Why Florida?" I was curious. I was from Florida. I had no idea why anyone would move here. I had heard a stand-up comedian refer to Florida as God's waiting room.

"It seemed like a good getaway. Do you miss your father? I know you say he was Satan and all, but really do you miss him? You never speak of him," Silka said.

"A good general indication. He was a pathetic individual. He poisoned me to get back at my mother, because he knew she would have to bear the brunt of taking care of me. At least for a time. He poisoned me a second time while I was in college, and it simply may have been because he did not want to pay for it. He had agreed in the divorce decree that he would pay for my college, but he weaseled out. My sister never went to college. She was a junkie at age fifteen and still is. I barely knew the man, except for his Satanic side was a little more overpowering and pronounced than most evil dads. I don't like men much. Huh, I wonder if there had been two of them."

"You mean like one was a step dad?" Silka asked. "Wouldn't you remember?"

"I don't know. I suppose it could have been like that. I wonder what my sister knows, but, no, there's really no use asking her. She's wasted all the time now."

"You could check marriage certificates. There might be a way to do that online, but then these records are probably in micro-fiche. Where would those be stored?"

"Probably Tallahassee. I had a doctor die when I was in therapy in Jacksonville, and no one could find my records, because he had them shipped and put in a warehouse in Tallahassee. Good luck finding them now. I was still working as a waiter then; it was later that I broke down my third time, and then you got to see me in all my glory my fourth major break. How did you hang in there?"

"It was tough. Especially when you started shooting up your old apartment. You nearly caught it on fire when you blew up the television. But I was not really that afraid that you would hurt me or Hinton. But it was obvious you were hearing voices. Will they ever go away?" Silka asked.

That she asked that particular question meant more in the world to me than anything. She wanted to help me with my suffering, and she had in so many ways, and she put forth the exact question I needed to hear, regardless that I didn't have an answer.

"I don't know. One day, they will go away forever. As soon as I am back on my home planet. Or at least if I hear them, I won't have some idiot psychiatrist telling me they are hallucinations."

"Well, I hope I get to keep you in the meantime," Silka said.

"You are such a blessing to me. I would say from God but He and I are not on terms anymore," I said.

"I never really believed in God. Why would this planet be so messed up if there was a God up there?" Silka said.

"He's real and that's his job, to screw things up and walk away. That is what he is designed for. Just nobody recognizes that, or not many of us. But then more and more are becoming aware. It seems everywhere I go now someone is switched on, a bunch of people now."

"What about your father then?" Silka asked, meaning my Satanic father.

I always used the term dad for my earth putz dad, and father for my satanic father, or they could have even been the same, just different sides of each other, which would make my dad an alien as well. And that might mean the real Satan who had visited me two or three times in my life was the real deal, and the fake Satanic side of my father was just a split personality of his. My dad might have been schizophrenic. Many doctors and therapists had referred to schizophrenia as split personality, but I guess it grew unfashionable to do so, but it is probably more accurate as labels go than using paranoid or hebephrenic as descriptors. All the varieties of schizophrenia blend into each other at times. I have a tendency toward catatonia too. After my second suicide attempt I was in a coma for three days, but that is really not the same as catatonia.

At any rate, getting a straight answer out of any family member was useless, and my dad had been gone from Florida for so long I didn't know anyone who knew him. They probably wouldn't know anything anyway, so it was kind of useless to try and find out information about my dad, and everything the CIA had on him was still classified, and as I said, I didn't have a security clearance.

"He's an alien from somewhere else, and he's been here a long time, so he's got a good grasp of things."

"Who's more powerful then?"

"God. But they are really in cahoots."

"Interesting. You definitely have strong beliefs. I'm going to turn in. You coming?" Silka said.

"Yes, darling. We are actually turning in at the same time now. I get cuddle time."

"Let's do it," Silka said.

Chapter Three

Silka had gone to work the next morning and I had taken Hinton to his play school. He had adjusted to this new place. He didn't like the first one he was in, a sort of recreational facility for challenged kids, but this next one I found in Orlando, he liked fairly well. I got coffee at my favorite coffee shop before returning home and spoke to the real Jenn. She was a beauty, with her blonde hair in pig tails and those fashionable eye glasses she wore. She was a smart gal too. I always caught her reading on her breaks, and she was about college age, but I don't think she could afford to go to college.

I had an academic scholarship to Grinnell, a full one. Everything but books. They even guaranteed me a job on campus, so I took whatever I could find most semesters, which meant the cafeteria usually. Those were the easiest jobs to find. I ran a dishwashing machine, because I did not like being in the line serving food. It was a big social scene in the cafeteria, and now as back then, people make me nervous. I prefer my easels and linseed oil, paints and brushes. That's why a woman like Silka is such a find. She's fifteen years younger than me, and I know that sounds like a trophy relationship, but I love her, and she can still put up with my attitudes and general craziness. She is beyond the "me, me, me" phase. I'm not fit to have another relationship, so if she left me, that might be it for me. I might be alone after that. But maybe not. I'm still waiting for that big killing in the stock market. I probably would have a trophy bride after that, if Silka left me. I guess I could hire a friend or two if I made a big splash on Wall Street. I'd settle for a nice little splash and the love of a good woman. That's all I really want: and I bet most men would agree, and most others, financial security and a relationship that works nicely most of the time is all there really is. And art. There is no real point to anything else. Except kids, I guess, but I missed that boat.

"How you doing?" I asked.

Jenn brought me my coffee and said all right. She said she was tired. Jenn was so perfect looking she looked starched. She just hung together so well.

"What would you do if you had done something great, Jenn, and no one knew about it, and you were a braggart by nature, but everyone knew this about you, and no one would be inclined to believe you anyway?"

"Simple. I would write a book. You paint, so try your hand at writing."

"What is your IQ, Jenn?" I asked.

"It's up there. I don't really know. Slinging hash is not my last job."

"Oh, I know that. You're brilliant. I'm going to miss you."

"Where are you going?" the real Jenn asked.

"Silka and I are moving to Jacksonville, I think." I was tempted to say Miami. That is what all the CIA members say. They cycle them in and out fairly regularly, and whenever a job is done for certain individuals, they say they are moving on to a bigger city. I guess that way no one can find them, wherever it is they go.

"I think I will. I'm a writer now too. That should fill some empty hours when I can't paint."

"All problems have solutions. They are just equations," Jenn said. You may not know the solution, or there may be a way of only partially solving the equation, but it's there for anyone that wants to do her homework." Then Jenn thought telepathically into my mind the words, *I love you.*

I thought back to her, *I know*, and I felt good. She loves me, and she has a boyfriend she is happy with, and she still loves me. I was not sure what I had done to encourage such a kind feeling. I smiled at her.

I went home and popped on my computer, something I had not done in a couple of days. I plopped down and began to write. It flowed out of me much more simply than I had guessed it would, but then I had all that pent up emotion and like the Jenn at the concert, who may have been my mother said, I would be in constant pain after I was finished fighting my fight. I sat down and wrote the following:

I know I come across as a pompous know-it-all with questionable class and am basically offensive to most people, but when you save a planet, or put in an effort that might lead to saving a planet, you have to tell someone. It's too big of a secret to keep, and it really shouldn't be kept at all, but one must be somewhat discreet, because there are varying and opposing factions at war on earth. They are not all so obvious either. I was bound to step on some toes. And I stepped on some pretty big toes. But then war is war, and Hell is Hell, and I'm never returning to either. I make that promise for right now.

I could start in some vein like Poe, and say you might think me mad, but I tell you the plan was all laid out. The truth is, however, I never had a plan. But there were two things I always knew would happen in my life, well, actually there were three things. I knew the government would come for me, that was terrifying enough, but I also knew my brain would be dissected. How literal or figurative the second matter was I could not say. The third thing I knew was that I was going to do something great. As I always claimed, something good, right and proper. I didn't know that would include slaughtering millions or perhaps billions of hostile alien combatants. But they were the invaders, not me. Earth is my planet and I leave it to the earthlings.

My motto had always been King, Country, and Wife, and as I am an American citizen, the CIA came as close to King and Country as I got, and well, I got divorced during this time from my wife, Alison, so I guess I screwed up some things for me personally, but my new family the CIA takes good care of me. They have kept me alive this long. I kind of hope that continues. Kurt Vonnegut said once, "no one has a life worth living and most of us have an iron clad will to live it." My iron-clad will was slipping away, but I suppose there were still bits and pieces of a life on earth that I appreciated.

It was only three paragraphs, but it pleased me, and I wanted to try and write more later. I wondered if I would ever finish an actual manuscript. It had taken a couple of hours to get that far, so I decided to push away from the computer and go see about lunch. An hour or so after lunch, I could negotiate with myself about whether I would paint that day or not. I might not be able to open the door to my studio and walk in, knowing I had work to do. I had a blank canvass set up in there, which is always so daunting, but I might think of some image in my mind that I could hold onto and mold into something fit for my oils. I rarely studied an image too long or worked on site. My style of painting, while considered realism, sprung from my imagination more often than not. I would draw in details as they came to me. I saw them appear in my mind in a layering effect. The longer I kept my mind open the more the layers went on while I sketched the scene. Then at some point, I would start painting. I never really knew when that would be. I never knew if I would finish a work or not either.

The film in my mind was similar to an astral transmission, and I don't mean of a space vehicle, (I am the least mechanical person on earth, and I'm only an average driver); it is more like a transmission of data, a steady stream, that when I can paint, it never lets me down. It is something like I hear writers speak of, as though God is telling them what to write, or a spirit or angel, or I guess a demon, perhaps. Aliens can do this too, I imagine. There is plenty of everything on this world, except for things that make sense.

Our science is relatively incapacitated, religion is just a code of chores, and the other alternatives like witchcraft and voodoo, while some are enticing from a spiritual standpoint, don't have much rhyme or reason and become things to dabble in only. The economy doesn't work anymore either. It's a feudal system, and we are slowly, gradually returning to feudalism, with serfs and Lords.

That is where I stepped in, and about half the population of the earth, because they all became imbued with some alien spirit, and those that possess the technology and know-how from some other, possibly distant, constellation or star scheme and all baguets, will have to join forces, or this entire rock dies. I get out of here soon enough, so I am going to sit back and have some fun. I guess the ship that has been looking for me all these years has finally found me, and I get to go home when I die.

It is unclear to me how many can get off the rock as well, so a concerted effort is required. And that means alien cultures are going to have work together. That could prove quite interesting in and of itself. A baguet, by the way, is a concept or what passes for a concept or anything that a concept might become. It also can be spelled like the French bread stick, a baguette, and means an oblong rod. An alien offered me that bit of insight and it has served me well. Her name was L. Just simply L. She liked to be called Dr. Laura, but I do not think she was the well-known therapist. I'll explain more about L and her husband Sir and any baguets later. One need not say related baguets, because that is implied in the use of baguets. In English, a baguet is roughly cut gem, and I think that applies reasonably well.

We won't understand the concepts by and large associated with baguets until sometime later in earth's history. It is not that the aliens that are present on earth at this time have been dumbed down, though some weren't really very bright to begin with, like the Shitheads. Earth putzes are being dumbed down at an alarming rate, but they are no longer in charge of their own destiny. Look at our space stations and space technology, most of which has come from very well-intentioned and bright by local standards earth putzes, but clearly has little chance of working. Certainly, there is a lot of technology at hand that only a limited few really know about, including some earth putzes, but most of it is not anywhere it needs to be to include a mass migration off this rock when it dies in about five hundred years. That's about 2508. Now I guess I sound like Nostradamus. I wonder what planet he was from.

So, I took it out of their hands because it was certain annihilation for earth beings and since I more or less inherited this planet, I would like to see the diversity that is here already continue to grow and prosper. It could be as soon as within the next couple of decades that more or less everyone understands the baguets they need to. The green revolution will slow things down in terms of the earth's destruction, but it is a stop gap measure at best. Over population is the key problem, and the best thing that could happen to earth is for a good-sized meteor to land in a populous area.

The next truly momentous year in earth's history is around 2028 or 2029, somewhere in there. It is a make or break year, but what happens I don't know. It might be a meteor. This year I reflect upon in large part is 2008 obviously, and I might as well go into explanation of what that year means. I am sure I'll get side tracked, so mea culpa. An alien female asked me if I knew the meaning of 2008; she was surrendering, but was kind of a bitch about it. But then she was the lead Goddess. I had met her in college, and forgotten all about her until one day, when I was in the backyard of my old house I shared with Alison, who was just an earth putz, happily so for me. So this voice booms from the Heavens, actually two of them, her lover's voice I could hear as well, and she says I had defeated her and her race.

She was a stylish, feline little creature in college, and I was supposed to have been wed to her or something, which didn't happen, because my earth putz dad poisoned me to cover up his sins and no one saw that one coming. Anyway, I was hanging out by my pool, and Nena, the lead Goddess, speaks in this familiar voice and I mean it boomed in and we talked a little bit. The conversation was no act of contrition on her part; she had a rather blasé, matter of fact tone that I had defeated her and the rest of her Goddesses. It was nice that my old house bordered a creek and had a huge concrete retaining wall in back, so my neighbors couldn't hear.

I was certainly cracking up, or so it seemed to everyone else, but I had finally realized my place in the universe, and I just had to let others think what they wanted. They really mattered less to me on that day, the horrible white trash and some of the otherwise nasty earth putzes, even though I fought for them. A soldier's fate. He fights for those whom he fights for. He or she does not get to choose.

I realized I am one of the original creators of the universe trapped in an earthly putz body, but sure as shooting I am an Immortal, and since so much does not become revealed to me until my next life, I don't have a lot of clues what that entails. One reason the CIA was defending me was because quite a number of alien species were after me, some of whom belonged to that infamous Russian organization known as the KGB and what was left of it. They were not much fun to deal with either, but the CIA has much smarter aliens.

I haven't even mentioned the plant people in my discourse as yet. I don't have any other name for them, because I have no clue where they come from and what plant species they have inhabited. The plant people have a definite fondness for well-groomed topiary. So do I.

But I am part of a family finally again, and not some putzy type family like I've got on earth, even though none of them, except my first to die brother, was truly a putz. But now I am a member of a family that can do some meaningful work and some good on a drastically backwards rock and help matters across the universe in general. I knew I was undertaking a huge responsibility, but it is one of the reasons I became aware again after so long, and I guess it was my time to do what I did. Even still, I was told I was in Hell for one hundred and fifty billion years. Fortunately, I don't have much recall of that in this life. I'm already an emotional cripple, but I am sprung from Hell. And anyone who tries to put me there, I'll beat him to the punch. I can switch a person off with a phrase.

Anyway, back to the meaning of 2008. I knew I would get sidetracked. There are two brothers, and somehow I became a third brother, but there always were the three brothers that created everything in all dimensions throughout all the universes, parallel and the known one at present. Which saying present and at this time or in the present are really meaningless, but they translate into some kind of understandable concept in English. And somehow I became a third brother, or like I said, I always was perhaps, and that has already happened in this life of mine with Silka and Hinton and my dear mother with Alzheimer's, which means I can be anywhere and everywhere in all dimensions, if I want to be. Or at least very soon I will be able to.

So Nena, the surrendering Goddess, asks me do I know what the significance of 2008 is, and I blow her off. I didn't know the significance, and I expected her to lie anyway, and besides, I had gotten over her a long time ago. The sex was not that great and she was very manipulative. She acted like her job was to cuckold me, and I wasn't interested.

I loved her in college but that was thirty years before, and while that seems a short time to get over the lead Goddess in the known universe, she always was kind of bitchy, even when she was surrendering to me. I bet Lee had nothing but civility for Grant. Hirohito was very subdued at the table as well, I have heard. So I just kind of figured out what 2008 meant. The 2 was for my two brothers and the double zeros were for God. He was the alpha and the omega, which is symbolized by double zeros.

I have to dwell on God at this point in the narrative, because He is such a royal pain in the neck. Because God tricked me and was tricked by the Goddesses, who played with his programming over and over to suit their own needs, He sequestered me in Hell for all those years. So, I put God in Hell myself after I became aware of who I am. I can still hear Him some times, but his voice grows fainter all the time. I hope to forget about Him soon.

The current sentence is one thousand trillion quadrillion years as measured where time goes by the slowest in the known universe. There are places in the universe where the equivalent of a year in terrestrial time takes centuries, millennia perhaps. He won't survive, so in effect I have killed God. Good riddance. I know this probably makes all the followers of Satan very amused, of which half the planet's population at this time belongs to Satan and is part of his army, but Satan had only a small fraction of anything to do with what I did. Satan needed a deal or he was going to be bound and probably gagged for all eternity, and that may be the only true statement in the Bible. God's word is fairly accurate, but who cares, or at least I don't, because none of it comes true because God killed Christ. God wanted his planet back and he had told everyone including Christ that Christ was his son. So he had to kill him, so there's no second coming of Christ. So, in a sense you could say I avenged Christ's death. Christ was probably a good guy, a little naïve most likely, but that's what happens sometimes. It is a dog eat lamb world.

So, the double zeros is the end of God. The alpha and the omega played out. Kaput. God is now just a heartwarming notion. Think of Him and feel good. That's all he was worth anyway. His job, what he was designed for, was to wreck everything, which I must add he was very good at. The 8 in 2008 applies mostly to my earth family, who have been around for a long time and all, except for my putzy brothers, came from somewhere else, and except for me, because I was already there. Some place else, I mean. I was everywhere or at least quite a number of places throughout the universe; I just didn't know it.

The eight represents the fake Satan, who was my father—and it turns out some alien jerk—my earth putz dad, who was not much better, but may have been an alien as well; my mother, who was the previous Queen of Creation in several older dimensions, and she became Nena in this creation. So that's two for her and two for my dad and father. My brother that was murdered by my dad was just an earth putz, so he doesn't count; my sister is actually a witch and a shape shifter, who are aliens, so she does count; and then there is me and the two I created. That is eight. One of my brothers, the one who died of a heart attack was just a warlock, so he doesn't count. The 8 in 2008 represents my family here on earth, except for the two I created, but they do count.

I call my two creations the Queen and Princess of creation of this the known universe at this time in the history of the universe and forward. And we keep the title so far into the future, which is really another of those meaningless terms, that no one knows what happens next. I think it goes something like that. I have already in this life joined my two, and my brothers, and probably I am a part of numerous other families around the universe, but those are not where my main consciousness lay. It is stuck on earth.

I created my two, not solely by my own hand; I had some help from both of them, and we struggled a bit here and there, especially in the beginning there was this huge jockeying for power, but we have come together nicely as a unit. The Queen of Creation is Rebecca, a dominant female, and our child is Chloe, the Princess of Creation. All of this part of the narrative took place in the year 2008 according to the Augustan calendar, and if you ask me the A.D. or anno domini, is pointless, because the year of our Lord ended when he died. There's no zero year on the

Augustan calendar, because it goes from 1 B.C. to 1 A.D. as though when Christ was born it began the year of our Lord. But Christ is dead, and if he did rise from the dead, I am sure he did not stick around. But there could be a second coming, if Christ really survived, and most Christians are putzes, so maybe Christ comes back to save the working families and the serfs on the earth. Maybe the meek really do inherit the planet. It would certainly let me off the hook, and then He could have this planet, because I'm sick of it here. Never time travel unless you are sure of the way home. That's where God tricked me too.

But that is the meaning of the year 2008. I reference years, days and hours slightly differently from most. B.C. is before coffee, D.C. is during coffee, and A.C. is after coffee. And AC/DC is a rock band. P.C. might wind up being post coffee, but because of all the pills I take, I still need a good umph of caffeine. That is how I count my days. And 2008 was the year of the rat in the Chinese zodiac, and I am a wood rat. It was a great year, but the brutality was a bit shocking.

I put in place some war toys that were used to viciously attack the Chinese, but I didn't know that was what they would be used for, so I plead ignorance and innocence on that charge. And I liked China when I visited. I hiked a good bit of the Great Wall. So, it was a tough year, 2008, a year of qualms and craziness, but look what I wound up with, an entire universe. I could not have anticipated such a good year, in spite of the constant pain that has begun. I hope the pain ends when I shake this body.

Chapter Four

One reason for the constant pain I found myself in can be easily attributed to the Shitheads. There are literally billions of them on earth, and many of them are as dumb as their moniker implies. They appear so dumb they can easily be taken for putzes, but putzes usually have a much gentler nature. The Shitheads are born and bred to fight, like pit bulls, so that never-say-die attitude that the Goddesses have the Shitheads have deeply ingrained in them as well. They have such sheer massive numbers that they can overwhelm very easily, but I found a key to their survival. I even destroyed their Imperial Wizard, who attacked me one night in the comfort of my own home. He was dressed in his sissy, ceremonial garb, a red frock with black collar, and he was taking everything out of my body. He was sucking everything right out of my body. I would have been a piece of a man, which I wound up being anyway, but there's some hope for recovery.

The Shitheads cannot tolerate freezing temperatures. So that is probably why most of the Shitheads are in warmer climates, as opposed to the Goddesses who like the colder temperatures. That also explains why there are so many Shitheads in the South.

And they attacked me mercilessly, but all I had to do was convince them that they were frozen, and a frozen piece of shit just crumbles into nothing. It took months to rid the universe of most of the Shitheads, especially the ones who attacked me on earth. They came from all over, millions, perhaps billions, of them. Not all Shitheads are stupid either, just the ones on earth mostly. And the smart ones around the universe saw a good opportunity to thin their ranks of the incompetent and idiotic ones, so they sent them off to fight on earth, and either I was going to win, or they were, and then the Shitheads would have had greater claim to the planet. I won, of course.

It was after lunch, and as I suspected I could not sit down to paint. I didn't even try. I didn't even go in my studio. I went back to the computer and decided that I would continue to follow the real coffee shop Jenn's advice and pound out my story and hopefully win some kind of award or sell a few dozen copies. I might enter it in some contest or actually pursue finding a literary agent, which finding one is almost an impossibility. I remember how grateful I was when Chanel took over managing my painting career. We had become good friends and she was able to coax me out of my post-divorce shell.

The CIA protected me from my enemies known as the Shitheads. The CIA detested the Shitheads, and so did many of the Goddesses, but they were largely intermingled and intermarried with the Shitheads, the Goddesses that is, in the South at least, so they existed in some form of co-habitation even before I did what I did.

The members of the CIA are brilliant, beautiful and brutal. The men are rough and tumble and the women will gut you like a pig if you stand in their way. It was they who probably had me beaten so far enough into submission that I had no choice but to willingly cooperate. The CIA has been focused on saving the planet for a great period of time, and they knew, or learned, I was their man, and they came after me with a vengeance. They insisted I move to Washington D.C., but I am a very casual and easygoing person, and the "yes sirs" and the "suits" were not for me.

So they chased me out of my city; I was living in Orlando at the time, and I followed the CIA as far as South Carolina before I sneaked out one night. Then they chased me to Texas, but I fought my way home. There were some scary moments in New Orleans with the Shitheads, but I made it out alive and back home. I was trapped near the levees with a bunch of Shitheads around me. I had turned off to get gas and got lost. But I had my reasons for wanting to return to Orlando. I was married and owned a house. I had bills to pay and a job to go to and I thought I had some friends, but none of that survived, except the bills and the house. The house was, however, the first casualty of the divorce.

On the drive into Texas along I-10, I felt a Shithead blow the back of my head off with a real gun and when I reached back there, there wasn't even a scratch. It hurt like Hell though. Mostly the Shitheads used some kind of stick that looked like a ruler to kill people. The black ruler was the highest form of this weapon, but it did not really have much of an effect on me. It was just a stick. And the people shot with this stick would actually be dead, but they wouldn't die in bodily form or in consciousness, if that ever happens, for a few days. Furthermore, they could walk and talk and function like they had before, and then a few days after being shot, they would keel over and die. As a result of being shot with a ruler so many times, I no longer have a left lung. My heart is probably damaged too, but my time is not up yet.

Another tactic Shitheads take is to sling shit in the eyes of those they felt to be inferiors, or those that they wanted to kill. If a putz, whom they rarely dealt with this in this manner, received too much shit in his eye, he or she would die or go blind eventually. And regular putzes had no idea this was even happening. No one spoke of these matters ever. It was all handled telepathically or by frequency. Different planets around the Milky Way Galaxy and beyond have different frequencies, and when someone is tuned in on a specific frequency he can hear everyone he or she outranks. An Alien named Sir told me that. He had no idea who I am. He thought I was from his home planet, and I may have been on his planet, but I wasn't from there.

Sir pretended to be God, but he wasn't the real God just a graven image with fewer powers, but he was a powerful alien and he outranked all the CIA, so the members of that organization could never determine whom I was talking to when it didn't make sense what I was saying. Sir was married to L. She set him up, because she wanted to be with her lesbian lover, Rita. Somehow L must have determined that I outranked Sir, or she peeked into the future, which is a meaningless expression, and saw that I defeated Sir and his comrades. I liked L, but she was kind of a strict dominant, which was okay, but I got a little tired of the beatings.

I was pleased. My first day as a writer and I had written something intelligible. Perhaps not intelligent, but then tomorrow was another day. It was time to go pick up Hinton and start dinner for Silka and me and Hinton. I felt like making enchiladas. I walked out to my car. The afternoon air was fresh and crisp, and it smelled pleasant, and the sunlight cascaded around me and lifted up my spirit a little. I had been so absorbed I almost lost track of time, but something caught me and held me out of that abyss. I used to always get yelled at by my mother whenever I was late. I had a bad drug habit during some of the time I lived with her, so I was late frequently to all sorts of affairs.

It is hard to say who is meaner: A Shithead woman or a Goddess. The Goddesses definitely win in the brains department, but then Shithead women are every bit as beautiful as the Goddesses, but since they conglomerate in the South, they are a poor match for education often. If you see a Shithead woman with a man and you ask why is she with him, the likely answer is he is a putz. The Shithead women breed with the putz men, and the Shithead line is handed down through the mother, so their children will be Shitheads too. The Goddesses and the Shithead women alike have their own men, which they keep them as lovers and concubines and companions and not much else; they rarely marry their own men, but on occasion they do. Shithead men are sometimes pretty boys, and the men that belong to the Goddesses are often fabulously well-coiffed and handsome and sophisticated.

The plant people and their gorgeous topiaries have handsome men as well, and though they are easy to confuse by their looks with Shithead men, they act completely differently, and not as Shitheads. The plant people seem to be part of the solution. The Shithead men and women don't seem to have figured this out yet—they need to be a part of the solution as well, or they might be left behind. So do the Goddesses need to understand this, and I have appointed or by rights of succession a new Goddess has taken over and I have faith, if there is such a thing as faith—or perhaps that is just an expression on my part—that this new lead Goddess will do the right thing by herself and her people and the universe we now live in.

Chapter Five

"They're shooting at me," I yelled. "Man, this hurts like crap."

"Just take it. They can't kill you. Remember, you're an immortal." My CIA scout and my two wingmen had chimed in those encouraging words. They weren't shooting with guns, but I was getting torn up all over the place. Everyone's brake lights on his car were Gatlin guns, spewing barrels of bullets. It was then and there I realized that the brake lights on cars, traffic lights, and train warning signals all fired bullets every which way at whomever it was they fired upon, and that seemed rather indiscriminate at best. And I was being hypnotized to look right into them. The eyes are the windows to the soul. Most would consider blindness to be one of the worst afflictions on earth. I have always been scared I would go blind in later life. It is a primal fear. But I was hypnotized, a cat in a trap. The lure of looking down a gun barrel was too strong. I could see the bullets reel off one after another. I couldn't look away. I was crying and I was going blind in my left eye.

If they whip shit, or bullets for that matter, into your left eye it is because they consider you a superior. Otherwise, they use the right eye. If enough of the Shitheads follow this procedure, they can blind just about anyone or even kill the person, but I would wash it all away when I got home. I could just simply say, "all shit out on the note," and as long as there was music playing somewhere, which there always is around me, if only in my head, I could cast the bullets, the shit, the stench right away from me. The disgusting shit in my eyes would come out in the form of a giant, transparent penis, and there might be several of them in there. Shithead women in particular give off a smell of raw sewage, if a man is interested in them. It is like their own personal pheromone or cologne. They can be every bit as beautiful as the Goddesses, as I have said, if you can put up with the drugs, the stealing, the lies, and the smell of sewage during sex.

"I've got to pull out. They are using hypnotism."

"I thought that was it. You can go now. We can handle it. Go on home El Capitan. Tomorrow is another day. You're riding with the big boys now," one of my wingmen said.

"Heading out. I'll pray for you. Ha ha!"

I veered off in traffic and headed back for my house, not that I wanted to go home, but I was in no shape to go anywhere else. My left eye was nearly closed. I was a fighter in a prize fight and my manager had just thrown in the towel. Like Rocky Balboa I first told him to slit my eyelids, but this time he wouldn't do it. So, I went home. I would most likely encounter Alison or some strange man's car in my driveway. Her extramarital curriculum was well pronounced by then. I had not met Silka yet, because I had not officially decided to end things with Alison, even though she was becoming increasingly sadistic. She now beat with me a leather belt any time she wanted. She had no compunction over wielding a steak knife near my face, even on the odd occasion company came over. Luckily, the leather belt was only on my ass, but it stung and the beatings were becoming more severe.

I didn't know if I had been on planet earth just then. It seemed a lot of the fighting took place on a stage designed to look like my home town, or at least partly look like my home town. I could tell by the creepy Shithead trees. They drooped and dripped moss or branches and hid the light, and the city never trimmed them in my neighborhood. Many Shitheads were affluent, and though I was still a hungry artist, Alison and I lived in a nice area of Orlando. It was fierce fighting this time. I took on some Warlord, and he was not happy about it. The G-forces alone upon me would have crushed an ordinary man.

I was told once there are positive G-forces and negative G-forces. I never understood the difference because they both hurt like Hell. I actually felt the G-forces give me a hernia, but it was gone the next day. I had a severe case of diverticulitis left over for the past several months. Even though I had not yet met the Jenn who was possibly my mother or some baguet, I fully understood about constant pain and discomfort, but then what soldier doesn't? The Shitheads had the G-forces at their disposal in my bedroom. Somehow a Shithead had broken in or been let in; it could have been someone as simple as a plumber or a roofer, or someone like that in some similar capacity, and Alison, the wife I was divorcing as I would soon meet Silka, let them in without thinking twice. They had taken in my house with them some form of alien technology, not a natural form on earth, and they could increase the G's while I slept. I felt like an astronaut and every bit as tortured as one.

A voice told me once I was at twenty G's and that proved I was an alien. Alison and I had taken separate bedrooms. The death knell was ringing loudly and clearly for my marriage of nine years. I no longer cared. I was in such constant agony, I anticipated walking away from everything, my wife, my job as a waiter, my house, my health. I could sign a quit claim deed on the house and give it to Alison, I could find another job when I was ready, and maybe start finishing more of my paintings, since I needed out; otherwise, I was surely going to die, and the Shitheads really would win without me striking a blow for earth. This planet belonged to me, so it was incumbent on me to fight for it. For how long I did not know, because I was getting tossed about badly.

Besides, the CIA needed me. I had a family, even if I only communicated with them telepathically across long distances perhaps. Most telepathic communications had a short range, but there were those that beamed in from all over, and I believed beyond the Milky Way. It had to do with the power of the mind. The CIA had tested my IQ at 203 or 204. Certain high ranking aliens in the CIA complained my mind hurt theirs it was so strong, and they could not sleep either. Medication was the answer, but not until the fighting was done. Meanwhile, those among the CIA that weren't fighting and they were everywhere in Orlando by this time, were swallowing pills by the handful, because they had regular jobs to go to and duties to perform. That was another method by which they kept their personnel confidential.

I went back to my home and packed my bags. Alison and I had just gotten back from Denmark. It was not a fun trip. I flew back by myself about a week before this latest round of tussles. I had broken down in the airport and starting babbling nonsense about there being no bomb. Flight attendants and pilots don't like to hear such things, even when it is in the negative. I repeatedly claimed I had been fighting the Mujahedeen. Maybe I was.

The flight was delayed out of New York for Orlando for five hours, and I sat there barely moving a muscle the entire time. I sat and waited on the cold floor. I was broke and it was either sleep in the airport or catch a flight I had already paid for. It was a brutal and excruciating length of time to wait, not knowing if the attendants were going to let me on the flight or call the police on me. Finally, the Captain said he would let me fly. I had sat quietly for fifteen minutes.

With all the voices screaming in my head that was maybe the accomplishment of a lifetime. There were some major Shitheads with my frequency, and they were angry I had escaped my plight in Denmark. My wife had handcuffed me to a radiator and turned on the gas in the small apartment. Alison was a putz, but she had friends whose suggestions she took often that had to be Shitheads. At one point in the five hour layover, and the plane was parked right at the gate the whole time, I dozed off and woke up screaming. People catching a flight don't care much for that behavior. I finally played it cool though, boarded my flight and as soon as it took off, my rigmarole about there being no bomb on board started gushing forth again. I could not control myself any longer. Not so oddly, the flight was not too crowded, which had more passengers in a greater state of unease I am sure. There was no way the ones in economy class with me could take me down, if needed. I am a large, strong man, older now and hopefully wiser, but travel is so tempting. I think I'll take up the rails, if I continue to travel.

Chapter Six

It was a cold winter's day for Orlando. The temperature must have been about 10 degrees Fahrenheit, and the sun shone brightly through the windows of the house. That eighty-five year old brick house had excellent natural light and the original hard wood floors. It was shortly after breakfast on a Sunday. Alison and I usually ate breakfast early. I could still get her to cook for me, even if it meant frying some huge hunk of steak she hoped I would choke on. Lately the coffee had tasted suspect. I think there was something in it. My guess was arsenic, but the CIA informed me it had been Hemlock. I supposed there was some dignity in being poisoned with Hemlock. It was better than rat poison. It put me in good company.

"Pull down your shorts," Alison commanded as soon as she was done with breakfast. She bent me over the kitchen table as she inspected my ass. "Go get the large dildo."

"Can we do it tonight? I just woke up."

"Go, get it now, bitch or I am going to beat you."

I went into her bedroom and got the large dildo. It wouldn't fit in me, and I knew she wanted to hurt me with it, but the alternative hurt more, so I would take as much of it as I could. She stripped the rest of my clothes off and took care of business. It felt like pressure that was ripping me apart from inside. Then she said for me to get dressed and not come home until sundown. She had hidden my car and door keys, and I guess I took too long, so she just turned me out with my shorts and a t-shirt and no shoes or socks. I would have to walk to the park about two miles away and sit there all day, and it was cold. If I went to a neighbor's, I would have Hell to pay. They would likely get involved and I could not risk that.

My friends had all deserted me, and though there were people in my community that guessed what was going on, Alison kept me away from anyone who was likely to help me. I had quit my job in lieu of being fired, and my social security disability wouldn't kick in for another six months or so. I didn't have a penny; Alison took my check from work every two weeks. She took my tips too. It went right into her bank account. I would short her on what I really had made for tips each evening, but she always found where I stashed the money. That was when I bought a safe and refused to give her the combination. I guess she had little use for me anymore, but she still had deep rooted needs that concerned me, like torturing me. But my career was starting to go places near the end of my marriage. That day in the park helped.

No money meant no lunch, no coffee, nothing. She had hidden my car keys the night before, so she obviously planned this one. I hadn't merely pissed her off; she now sought ways to torture me. She was waiting to see what I would collect from my dying dad, the putz, and if there was anything she could wrest from me, but I had a plan for that money. Unfortunately, either my sister cut a deal with the attorney or there really was nothing left of his estate. My sister, Dinah, the heroin-addict, had wanted to kill me, so maybe dad was just broke and there was no money, and I was sinking deeper and deeper into a pit of Hell that I saw no way out of. It was around then I tried to commit suicide the first time. The second time I lay in a coma for three days. It was kind of cool to come out of a coma. How many people can say that?

I could go to the park with the three fountains. There most likely would not be anyone there. I routinely avoided people now. I could not look them in the eye I was so ashamed of myself. The park with the three fountains was a little further away and about a mile down from a first park. The nearer park was across from a church, and while Christians were okay with me, not that I enjoyed the Baptists very much—so many of them were actually Shitheads—I could not exactly throw myself on the mercy of church goers, seeing as how I am the reputed son of Satan. Everyone in my little few square miles knew me or knew about me. By turning me out, Alison was hoping I would get Baker Acted, a little piece of Florida legislation that allowed police to hold suspected mentally ill patients in a hospital without arresting them, but since it was a Sunday and there was not much traffic, I didn't spot any police officers. It is merciful legislation. I chose to go to the farther away park with the three fountains, known affectionately by the locals as the duck pond.

I would have to travel through Shithead territory to get there, but there was a better chance of being left alone once I got there. I could do ten hours on a bench. It's not that different from a cell or solitary. The benches were metal. They would hurt my ass and be cold. Insult and injury do go together. The trees on my street hung down forming a dense canopy that blotted out the light, and even though the sun had been up for an hour or so, it seemed dark and dank, as if I was entering a jungle.

I called upon my two. They were the two warriors that protected me whom I had created. I referred to them as my F-44 Hornets.

"Where are my F-44 Hornets?"

My two whooshed past my left and right ears at the same precise moment. They were in formation and might have been present already, and though I can see invisibility, I wasn't looking for them. My spirits picked up. Nothing could harm me now. "Let the Shitheads bring it," I said out loud. My girls giggled.

Rebecca, I love you, I said.

I love you, Chris. It was a telepathic communication, but the message was very clear.

Chloe, I love you, I said.

I love you, daddy.

Do you want to fight?

Chloe spoke up first. *Let's play first, daddy.* They dragged out their light sabers and started cutting branches off trees, and I heard the branches crack and saw the branches fall to the ground on a blustery day. *We're landscapers, daddy.*

I laughed. Landscapers are usually Shitheads, especially if they are handsome. And they are everywhere in Orlando. Entire neighborhoods of individuals and families belong to the profession of mowing yards, and they earn their meager, seasonal earnings, cleaning up other people's yard debris. I wouldn't mind that so much, and I really didn't at all, but they have a tendency to be so conformist and such unreasonably confined thinkers. And where there is one Shithead, you can bet there are a dozen more close by.

Chloe was getting mischievous. She shaved an old stately oak into the form of a pit bull with jaws open and gaping, fangs poised to attack. I had to laugh. Some days my two were the only ones that made me laugh.

Daddy, there's some shoes on that man's front steps. Sure enough there were. I had never stolen a thing in my life, and I was certain this was going to come back to haunt me, and Chloe probably knew that—she was designed to be able to peek around the corner of time—and she loved to see me get in trouble. And she loved getting me in trouble. It was intensely funny to her, but then my feet were freezing.

Rebecca? I called.

Do it, Chris.

I looked to see if any cars were in the driveway. There weren't. I decided not to check the garage. I strolled over casually and picked up the shoes off the front steps. I needed them more than the owner at this present moment. They were tennis shoes and smelled like sweaty feet, but I would not be a chooser and they fit me well. I carried them away from the scene of the crime and put them on before I arrived at the duck pond. We had marched, myself practically naked, right through Shithead Central and not gotten a scratch. The Shitheads had kept their distance. When the Shitheads came home from church they would have some nice new topiary compliments of my two, and the plant people might enjoy what I was doing to further gentrify the neighborhood. Maybe some plant people would move in. The economy was in poor shape and houses were going for a song and dance.

I arrived at the duck pond and there was no one around, but there was a disturbing sight. The three fountains were on, blowing mists of water thirty feet into the clear blue sky, but as the water cascaded and just before it landed on the russet pond water beneath, holograms that appeared demonic in nature jumped away from the fountains and were unleashed. I was not particularly interested. Holograms can do definite damage though. To the unsuspecting, the holographic image will invade a home and establish residence there until it is encouraged to leave. They spit on people, they choke them, rattle things about and sometimes they carry swords or staffs and prick individuals' insides. These holograms at the duck pond were polite and knew to keep their distance. It is a simple matter to get rid of a hologram or shadow that might be wreaking a little havoc in your car or home. I just convince them they have done a good job and they can go back from where they came, which is Hell more often than not.

Shitheads like water too. It makes them feel all runny and gooey, I guess, so they use water to regenerate. That is one reason so many of our rivers and lakes and ponds are so polluted. The Shitheads can dissolve in water and then if the percentage of shit in the water is high enough they can reform and become a human likeness again. Every time this happens, the Shithead grows stronger and meaner. Some of them do this on a daily basis. I would hate to see what their bathrooms look like. The bathroom is a prime location for their activities.

Most of the universe was made of shit at one time, the first parallel known universe was at least. I don't know if the first parallel universe was pushed right or left when I separated it from the known universe of that time. I don't remember. I am not sure it was I who separated it from the known universe. The universe en todo is a glowing green grid in spherical form. The grid contains the parallel universes, and what is outside the grid I have no idea. That is probably where the true secret of creation is waiting to be discovered, but I don't know any way of getting there, and I wouldn't try. It could be nothingness or if I retained my consciousness in any form like it is now, it could be a place where nothing made sense. Some secrets are best kept till the proper time. The parallel universes, of which I have said there are about forty or forty-five in all, have to be pushed left or right before they can be pushed up to the top or down to the bottom. The older ones are top and bottom, and they are some freaky places.

The plant people are in either the top or the bottom. I can't remember which now. Everything is off in the plant people's universe, or their original universe, if that is where I was, and it is not off by much, but enough for one to know he's not in Kansas. The police cars in the plant people's universes do not have flashing blue lights, so I would just speed by them in my rocket car, a souped-up Honda, and the police could never catch me or get me to stop. Truthfully, I knew I was in a parallel universe, but I didn't know those were cop cars I was running from. All right, that's a lie. I suspected, but I wasn't sure I was running from the police. I thought they were, most of them anyway, ordinary variety Shitheads.

Many of the police are Shitheads, but they have a tough job to do, so I have respect for them. The times I was Baker Acted, and this idyllic day in the park was not one of them, the police have treated me fairly well. If you are mentally ill, you definitely want as little to do with the police as possible. The mentally ill are much more likely to have matters that involve police officers than any other government agency, but still I found the cops were fairly understanding. When I learned I could switch Shitheads into putzes, which was not on this idyllic day, I made a solemn oath to leave the police alone. Their job was too tough and dangerous without my stirring the pot.

If one travels through a parallel universe from the top, he has to come down through the left side of the universe as you would face it in your mind, or your mind's eyes, and all baguets. Then there is a divided highway of sorts that links the left side with the right side of all the universes, like a corpus colossum in the brain, and every so many spaces there is an opening, and you have to travel that road, the corpus colossum, which moves very quickly and one has to jump off at a proper landing point to cross from a parallel universe to another more recent one and then on and on to the known universe.

That is how time travelers used to get around the various universes. But as Einstein figured out the equation for the fourth dimension, I set about for my robots the task of solving the equation for the fifth dimension. Einstein said in his theory of relativity that the fourth dimension is time and it bends back on itself. So, my argument then became that the fifth dimension is thought and all baguets.

There were sophisticated entities looking for the answer. I knew the question and I alone apparently solved the riddle of the answer, but I had nothing in between, not one bit of the equation. But that part needed to be solved by mathematicians and scientists, not me. I assume it was, but I have no proof as yet. That comes, perhaps, in the next life, unless I am turned out to pasture, which suits me fine. I might still get an answer and be able to retire. But all one would need to do now to time travel is think himself or herself into the proper dimension and then back home again.

I set the Royal Guard, who are my personal robots primarily tasked with protecting me, but having very advanced capabilities as unseen the likes of here on earth, onto solving the equation, and then someone came up with a mathematical interpretation of the question. The Guard had helped too, but now when I get off this rock I have every expectation that travel in five dimensions is widely available for time travelers now. We will actually be able to travel in and out of our thoughts and all baguets. That might explain the blinking lights I see when I close my eyes. The time traveler sort of blinks out as if he is being teleported somewhere, but with no apparatus. So, a point of departure, or for that matter, a chosen destination is irrelevant. You simply think yourself into the proper space and time you want to be in once you arrive at the proper universe.

You can't broach a parallel universe through relativity alone. The only way to do that is if you go through a worm hole at the end of a black hole. I think that is possible in some form of craft, but how to avoid being crushed and escape with your consciousness is tricky. If you miss your mark in the fifth dimension, you take out on foot or by any vehicle and change the scenery around you until you are when and where you want or need to be.

I wandered around the park a little. I had grown up on a shady bit of street in Jacksonville, when my dad, the putz, was still in my life, and before I was raped the subsequent time by a friend of the family at age ten, and as I passed the Shell station that was near the park, which was missing the letter S, and had the word HELL emblazoned in bold, capital letters, I simply turned that stretch near the park into my old country road where I had grown up.

I used to call it sliding, but a silly television show claimed the name and concept, and though they had an idea of how it was done, the actors on the show could never get back to present day earth, so I lost interest. The show was cancelled early on anyway. It became more of a parody of itself with each viewing. I wanted the actors, who began to remind me of the crew on Gilligan's Island, to get back to earth, so I would have a notion how things might turn out here, but they had to keep sliding and got further and further away just for some ratings. It was shameful. The actors could have brought home some useful twig of enlightenment to this dismal rock, and then gone out in search of more, all the while sliding to the neatest places, or the most despicable ones, in the parallel universes. I realize it was a television program, but many ideas on earth are born this way. Hollywood probably has the densest conglomeration of aliens anywhere on earth.

But that is not really what sliding is used for. Sliding is much more time-oriented than it is space-oriented and pertains to changing time and circumstance in a relatively narrow line and timeframe of existence. One slides to set up better opportunities in one's life or get out of bad fortune, and it has much less to do with hopping around the universe. At least here on earth that is what I have found it useful for. And true we are sort of the last gas station before a few million light years of desert, so sliding here may be a limited concept. There may be some need of proximity involved.

I walked around one end of the park and coming through an opening in the brush, there were three lovely young ladies, athletic, tall, thin, dressed in stylish clothes with expensive, eye-catching jewelry, watches, rings, earrings, that were moving in the direction of a bench to sit on. They looked magical, like sprites, so lithe and graceful. I had looked into Heaven once and seen the sprites flying about. They washed windows and flew very quickly and fucked almost constantly. It was then I knew why I loved the Goddesses so much. The Goddesses, whom these three were, are promiscuous women, and they toy with their male lovers and husbands, and keep them on a leash, and the main reason they are able to do so is because the Goddesses are quite exquisite in bed. The prettiest of the three called out to me.

"Do you have any bread? We want to feed the ducks." She was completely unabashed about talking to a strange man. I had a scraggly three day growth of beard and a forlorn look in my eye, but they knew they had nothing to fear. The Goddesses are adept defenders; otherwise, they would never have conquered a universe. The prettiest Goddess had long brown hair and brown eyes, and she reminded me of my favorite Goddess from college, a Romanian woman named Nicola. We had shacked up our sophomore year after she transferred in from Swarthmore.

"Uh, no. I barely have clothes," I said piteously.

"Why don't you have clothes?" another Goddess spoke up. "Aren't you cold?"

"I had to make a quick exit from the house." I tried to make it sound like I was doing someone else's wife, when in reality it was more likely the reverse situation was true, and someone was going to fuck my wife, but the Goddesses could read my mind and I am more or less programmed not to lie too much. I thought telepathically into all three of their minds, *my wife turned me out*. The prettiest of the three reached out her hand and said, "Hi, I'm Chanel."

"My pleasure I am sure. I'm Chris."

Why did your wife turn you out? Chanel thought into my mind.

Because she has her lover coming over, I guess, and I would crimp her style.

"So what do you do, Chris? Do you have a job?" the one Goddess who had not as yet spoken said.

"I paint."

A chorus of appreciation went up from all three of them. The Goddesses are cultured women. "I own a gallery in Winter Park, Chris," Chanel said. "I would love to see your work." She took out a business card from her designer bag and wrote down her number and handed it to me. Call me. I'll arrange a consultation.

"Are you any good?" one of the Goddesses asked.

"I am," I said. "And I am not just saying so. I've sold pieces. How soon could you get me a showing, if you like my work?"

"Oh, a month or so. It takes a little while to get the press out and mix the vegetables. Do you have that many pieces? Enough for a show?"

"I've got about forty that are finished."

"That would do for a nice start," Chanel said. *I am looking for a new lover. It's my rules though,"* she thought telepathically.

Yes, ma'am, I said. "I'm in the middle of getting a divorce very soon I think. So I might just get my pieces and get out."

"Oh, I'm sorry. Marriage just doesn't work anymore." The Goddesses were all young, except Chanel who was closer to my age than the other two, and how the younger, pretty blond Goddess with the turned up nose and sparkling white teeth would know that the institution of marriage is a failed one, I had no clue. But they have these wonderful Borg-like minds, and they know things it seems impossible for them to know. I could tell Chanel was an experienced Goddess and that she outranked the other two. When they are children they tend to be very precocious. And I knew Chanel's rules meant her rules, but I hoped she was not too strict. With the Goddesses one has to pay attention to everything they say, because they mean the words that usher forth from their sensual lips. I wanted her to take me home that day, but I would have to go through the formality of auditioning my work and selling my soul to her. The deal was not yet set in stone. I had to prove I was worthy.

The Goddesses eventually got bored and left and I sat there on the bench and dreamed of what had happened in my life. It was not so terrifically great what I thought of, and I was still having flashbacks to times more painful.

I met Sir, the alien who pretended to be God, or God's silent partner in their war against the earth, and I thought he was the actual living and breathing God, who is ninety percent bolts and wires. Sir's voice boomed right into my home one lonely night. I was sitting at my dining table, alone, depressed maybe, perhaps even waiting for Alison to get home. She liked it if I was waiting at the table when she got home. I, of course, never knew when she was coming home and it grew later and later by every day, so I just wound up sitting at the table for hours doing nothing. I was collared and penned.

And one of these times, Sir said something about my birthright, like I was the Christ or something, which I knew right away was a lie, but his voice was so powerful. I tried to get up from the table and run into the family room, and he commanded me to sit down and pray to him. He was kind of a putz. I had to kill him. I stuffed him in Hell for longer than I did God. At least I made his sentence longer. He's still there now, and I can see him. Hell, in the case of Sir was a multi-disc CD player with room for one hundred and one CD's, that every time the disc changed it flashed three orange lights, which I am sure are intensely hot bursts of light. It was in the family room of my old house, so I sat there a lot and listened to music and tortured Sir, who was not God, but a God look alike.

But I was not the one playing Sir, his wife was. Her name simply was L, I have said. I never called her Doctor Laura, which she asked me to, but she didn't really mind that I didn't.

Sir and L were along on my little spaced out driving trip in my Rocket Honda. I traded it in on a Caddie after Chanel got me my first big showing. After a while the insanity got so bad, I just took off from my home and wife and job. I paid for everything with credit cards. The first time I took the driving tour it included the CIA, Satan, and my two, and my dad and father, and many of my father's associates, who were basically demonic, but really putzy ones, and, of course, Sir and L, and Rita, L's lesbian lover. There were a lot of aliens along for the ride.

I stayed in a bunch of dive hotels from Austin and Shreveport to Jackson, Mississippi to Nashville and Colombia, South Carolina. I was in every southeastern state and as far west as Texas. The CIA especially wanted me to travel to Austin. They are famous there. I thought I had entered another deep pit of Hell and was sufficiently floundering about, but the only really bad thing that happened was in Gadsden, Alabama, where a drug dealer flattened my tire. My cell phone had been stolen, but I had Triple A. and made a call from a restaurant, and was back on the road in the middle of the night in no time. I traveled a good bit at night, and I don't really know how I did that because I didn't have my glasses, and I am almost night blind.

I didn't know what I was running from; I guess the KGB had renewed its efforts in Orlando, and I kept getting farther and farther from my home. It was quite a struggle to get back home, and I fought off varying degrees of aliens and attacks to get back to my home. When I returned home, Alison never asked me where I had been. No one did, but then I didn't have a friend left in the world at that point. I was all alone and I was scared. I had not yet realized that I don't check out from this planet until the perfect moment, which I guess means when the ship gets here, but then lately I am informed from time to time the ship is here, and my good fellows are waiting on me. I hope they are having fun in the meantime. Some of them are in desperate need of fun, so I hope they have that opportunity. What constitutes fun for them I am not really sure. I know the shoot out at OK Corral with the Gatlin guns for brake lights was a lot of fun for them. Why should my family merely apply its brake lights when the members can use them as an instrument of destruction on a widespread basis to get even with certain aliens and avenge me. The aliens fired upon me, and my true family fired back.

They had a blast and they were always polite, and asked if they could join in the fun because earth is still my planet. Of course, there was no way I would ever turn down a request for fun. We were in South Florida when I realized a lot of my family was already on earth. I am still kind of a putz in many ways and slow on the uptake.

I wonder if Jim Carrey and I get to board the same ship. He might stay on earth longer than me; he seems to be having fun. He also knows how to get off this rock, I think. I wish I did, but then I know my ship is waiting. I wonder if it will look something like a tractor beam sucking my soul out when I die. I have always felt I die alone, so I guess that little bit of evidence will get overlooked.

Chapter Seven

Silka and I had decided to pack our gear and move to Jacksonville within the next two days. Silka had lined up a job through the Internet and her employer needed her right away. It was a temporary position with Merrill Lynch that would last five months and had the chance of going permanent. She might have the chance to study for her Series Seven license and become a broker. We were abandoning our furniture. We simply would leave most of it behind. There was not really that much, and nothing we could not replace easily enough. We would pack what we could in the two automobiles she and I owned and find an apartment in Jacksonville. I knew there were only two zip codes worth living in, in Jacksonville, and they were relatively small ones, so apartment shopping would not be that difficult, if things had not changed a lot. It had been twenty years since I had lived there, but surprisingly the areas we investigated seemed hauntingly the same to me.

The city was trying to revitalize the downtown area and along the riverfront and had made the apartments and condos so small, no one with a goodish-sized house in the suburbs was the least bit interested in buying. Only those from out-of-town were likely to buy such small homes. Even with the current trend of downsizing, the condos and apartments downtown were too small, some of them only five hundred square feet. Until we found a place, we would stay in one of those weekly rental places until the apartment was ready if we had to wait on the apartment complex's maintenance crew to clean up or paint or some detail like that.

Silka had given notice at the boutique. I had told Chanel, who was by then my personal manager for my artistic career and not my lover, that I was moving, but it was only a couple of hours north and on the coast. Orlando could not offer a change of seasons or the ocean. It was a new year by a few days, and Silka and I wanted something different for ourselves. We planned possibly as well on finding a little cottage on the beach. She would have to fight the traffic to work and home again, but for the ocean at our backdoor she was more than willing. She had always dreamed of a small house by the sea. The rent would be high, but for now it was the off season, so rates would not be so crushing.

We had outgrown Orlando. It was a huge tourist destination and so Disney-filled and with all the incumbent frills of Disney-like companies, and with screaming putz children and bad drivers that we dreaded going out anymore. Jacksonville is a slower pace—still a cow town—but the beaches are lovely. We knew a spot that I had showed Silka one weekend where we could take Hinton and he could actually live there and come home on weekends if we wanted. The extra socialization and attention would be good for him. Silka came up with the idea before I showed her the camp-like atmosphere of the special children's home, and she had toyed with the notion of placing in a similar home for about a year or so. She had hit a wall with her job. I was in another dry spell as concerned my painting. And Hinton was just too much for Silka to take care of, and for me, even though she took care far more of his needs than I did.

While my computer was still setup I decided to get some writing done. I had an angle to my story now. I guess a theme, I would call it. I had a controlling idea anyway. Socrates said a story is not about a single character or a series of events as one may think, but about a single event. Plot is about one event. That is why it is so significant to readers because they wonder, if the story is interesting, what the resolution to that single event will be. Since I had saved this planet and bequeathed it to the putzes, I had decided I would write about that as my event. So, I launched in and kept fairly busy with it the next couple of days until it was time to pack up and go.

It was one billion years in the future and I was still wandering about the earth and in human form. I looked, I guess, very much like I always had. I had dropped some weight. I thought for sure I would have checked out by now, and gone to a different planet, and maybe I had, but I was back on earth. Grudgingly so. There was a war going on between the United States and Mexico. Apparently cars were shooting at each other in the drive-thru lane of a McDonald's. The United States had been invaded. I was up on the hill above the violence, which was very peculiar, the hostilities, to say the least. It was not with bullets or guns; the cars seemed to be shooting or propelling some invisible projectile that was killing the person or people in the car in front of them. The technology seemed the same as from before. The earth stood in total arrested development. And the same cars kept going around and around the McDonald's and through the drive-thru. Well, it was a busy McDonald's and it was about lunch time, so killing someone in line in front of you was probably standard procedure on the planet by then. I hoped so.

I had just been released from an alien lockdown because I had tripped the virtual door and the CIA came running in when I did and took over the place. Of course, these gentlemen knew I was one of their own, and they had been looking for me, and looking for the door, but couldn't find it until I tripped it and forced it to open. The aliens had the newsman Anderson Cooper trapped in lockdown with me. He told a bunch of pointless stories and I really could not understand him. I found him a jovial, likeable guy though.

So, the CIA got me out of that mess of an alien lockdown, and as soon as I could I left and walked off. They might have slaughtered all the aliens inside. I don't know. I hope so. I knew I didn't want to be there, so I just strolled right out the front door, and no one said anything to me because of the commotion inside the building. So I wound up near this dumpster by the McDonald's near Florida State University's main entrance in Tallahassee. I had been catching a cab to San Diego, but we stopped for a soda, and I told the driver to go on without me. That was before the alien lockdown. I paid him two thousand cash for the ride. I didn't have any shoes, any money, and I hadn't shaved the entire time I was in lockdown. The aliens in the alien lockdown had stolen everything from me. I hadn't showered either. None of the aliens would let me, and the toilet reeked of urine and shit.

I knew one of the employees serving food at the McDonald's. He was a member of my troop. We had run a raid on Washington DC together to get some key people for the United States government released from lockdown. That was why the CIA was trying to get me to come to Washington, but I wouldn't go. In the long run, it was better that I didn't. We came through for them, I and my friend Yak, which is short for Yakuza. The Yakuza are the Japanese mafia, and they worked for me for a time. The CIA turned their heads the other way because I had enlisted the Yakuza's aid since they are well known for brutal tactics, and they helped me out quite a bit. You cannot catch a member of the Yakuza if he is on his motor bike. It's impossible. So Yak gave me a free coke. He said I could have anything I wanted, but all I wanted was a coca-cola. It was August, and hot as Hell. So, I took my coke outside and sat on the curb and I watched the war. It wasn't going that well for the United States.

I wondered if I was seeing some part of my future, as though I become embroiled in another war here on earth, or it was some kind of trick and I had been placed a billion years in the future. More likely, my family wanted me to see that this rock is doomed, and they wanted me to figure out a way off of it and back to my present time, which was the year 2008. The way I know, or at least think it was my family, was because of whom I met. There were a number of time travelers around the McDonald's. I was standing there outside the McDonald's and watching attentively and who comes up to me, but Jim Carrey. He's smoking a virtual jay. It was marijuana, but not really. It was just paper, but it smelled really good, and I wanted a hit off it, which I am sure he would have given me, but I have to watch my D2 receptors in my brain. They are the ones that regulate dopamine uptake and production, and marijuana increases my dopamine levels so I have to stay away from it. I can actually hallucinate for days from smoking one puff of marijuana. That sounds like a good thing, but really it's not.

Jim and I didn't really say much. He blew the smoke in my face, and it caused me to relax considerably. I had been crying because at that point in space and time I had to figure out how to get to Orlando and home with no money. They had stolen my wallet in the alien lockdown. I had no cash for anything, and not even a credit card. And the drive was over three hours by car.

The food in an alien lockdown is not real either. Neither is the air. So it took some adjustments being on the outside again. I had dropped about twenty pounds and I felt fairly good, but I knew I looked terrible. Anyway, I tell Jim I'm going to hit the highway because a plan was forming, and I compliment him by telling him he's held up well. He looked like he always did, in the prime of life. I think he's an immortal too. He has to be. And I feel certain there are not that many of us, so we must all be from one family. He smiles at me and says thanks, and I walk off, and that was my and Jim Carrey's moment one billion years in the future. Personally, I hope I am not there, and not under those circumstances ever again, and it is possible that one billion years in the future has already come and gone. I hope I get to retire. McDonald's must have served a few quadrillion burgers by then. That reminds me of that Woody Allen movie, "Sleeper." That was a fun bit of hilarity.

So, I go around the corner, and the CIA who has been communicating with me telepathically all this time says they are sending a car. "Do it soon," I say. "I need a ride home. Someone has to give me a ride or else I am trapped again."

"We understand, Chris, but we have to get you checked out first."

"Just take me home and then we can decide all that," I said.

"We know a place, Chris. Trust us. They will be glad to see you."

"Okay, I trust you guys." That was a hard phrase to utter. It was not an alien lockdown again. It was a CIA-run hospital. They got me ship-shape and gave me a bus ticket back to Orlando and got me in touch with a new psychiatrist there. My old one had been doing a rather shabby job of things.

Moving day arrived. I told my apartment manager we would be checking out on a permanent basis on Friday afternoon. She said just bring by the key that day and give her an address and she would mail any refund for the deposit. We planned on leaving a number of items behind, and the deposit was only two hundred dollars, so we didn't expect much to be left after they hoisted our furniture out to the trash. Furthermore, we planned on leaving Thursday night to avoid a confrontation. Our lease was up and we had gone month to month and we were paid up, so it seemed the apartment manager and maintenance would experience only minor inconvenience because of us. We left the door unlocked and the key on the table in the dining room, and headed out the door. It was so long Orlando. It's a putzy city anyway.

Silka and I had difficulties once in Jacksonville. Her job through the temp agency never fully materialized. The manager there kept telling her to come in the following week, and she explained she had moved from Orlando to accept this position, but that argument was to no avail. The guy at the temp agency seemed to be a Shithead. It would likely be back to retail for Silka, and she hated that industry, but there were a fair number of boutiques and interesting places that sold clothes and bric-a-brac at the beaches in Jacksonville. I had enough money to float us for as long as it took, but Silka was a strong independent woman and did not like being tied to my apron strings. She wanted to work, and I knew it would not take her long to find something.

We started getting the local newspaper, which was a significant embarrassment for the city of Jacksonville. The Times-Union was a redneck right wing rag, and a lousy one at that. The local news broadcasts were filled with hicks and rubes. There seemed to be a lot of Shitheads in town. I was having shit slung in my eye all the time. It happened so often, in fact, that my left eye, which denotes I am a superior to the one slinging the shit, became infected. Jacksonville was just another cow town, but we had chosen to carve out a niche here and find a slower pace of life. Believe it or not there was not a stitch of traffic on Sunday mornings. These putzes and Shitheads and the odd few Goddesses were all in church. We felt like we had the city to ourselves. Walking the beach on a Sunday morning became a favorite past time for the two of us. The religious factor, who were mostly right-wing radicals, did not even realize they were praying to a dead God and a Christ that was never returning. Baptists. They are about as dumb as it gets.

One Sunday morning I was out and driving, re-familiarizing myself with Jacksonville, and looking for a small shop somewhere I could set up as a studio. Having a studio in my home was not working for me anymore, and I reflected upon what had happened just about the time I met Silka. I was clandestinely sneaking behind Alison's back to see Chanel for about the last couple months of my marriage, though Chanel and I had not had much in the way of sex, but I figured what is good for the goose is good for the gander. Alison had her lovers and she did not even try to hide the fact anymore, and after a certain point she had begun to poison me with Hemlock, so I knew it was time to move on. Nothing spells divorce like Hemlock.

But this man had come to visit me when I still lived with my wife. I had remembered him, a nasty gay pedophile, who, in my opinion only took up space on the planet. And wasted space at that. He had come to unburden his soul, and not for any other real reason. He did not seek to make things right between us, nor could he have; he merely wished to get matters off his chest, so he could feel better. It turns out he was dying from cancer, and involved with a twelve step recovery process, and somewhere in there, around step nine or so, he looked me up and decided to tell me he had raped me at age ten.

I cried when he told me this. And so did he. But not a single tear of his was for me and what my life had become and what he had helped it to become in the process. I could feel the steel bars close around my heart. Furthermore, he never said he was sorry. I thought that was part of the twelve steps, openly admitting the hurt you had caused and begging for some semblance of forgiveness.

What a marvel of manhood this gay pedophile was. I had heard it rumored he traveled to South America quite often as it had been easy to obtain little boys for his purposes. A small town and a hungry family is all it took. I actually thanked him for coming clean with me as I said it, and wished him a safe passage home, and secretly prayed this excuse for whatever it was that he stood for, would rot in the worst pits of Hell for all time.

My life had ended at age ten. Everything I had lived until the year 2008 was a complete lie. That encompassed a little less than four decades. When the man, if one could refer to such an abomination as he with such a term, left, I openly wept. I cried tears for myself. The agony I felt. It was as if I had been thrust straight back into Hell. It was the first time I had cried in twenty years, other than earlier in the year 2008.

As I began reliving that moment in time, the tears filled my eyes so much I had to pull over in the car during my search for a studio. I was blinded by hatred and fear of what I might do and what might become of me. I was quickly turning into a misanthrope. Luckily, I was not a misogynist. I still saw purpose for women and enjoyed their company usually. But I was developing an intense hatred for men. I do not suppose that is so rare among men. It is quite common among women I understand.

Women do more good in this world. I would have to except my family from that statement, but as a generalization I think it is apt and holds water. I suppose many men hate other men. I suppose this was at the root of my fighting and fisticuffs and otherwise banging heads with other men, because I detested them, and I could only be pushed so far. I felt they were an inferior species. Most men are Shitheads anyway; they are mere pests to be rid of. In that instant, I felt like an animal. This man had stripped me of what was decent in me or what had a chance to become decent in me, and left the carcass by the side of the road with its pants down. And at my age of ten years old.

My putz earth dad, the psychiatrist and Naval Captain, had done something very similar on his deathbed. He had told me that he had hypnotized me, and I had moved closer to him with an incredulous stare in my eyes, that must have threatened him because he clammed up and refused to tell me why or what the hypnotism might have entailed. How had these people done these things to me? And what purpose did it serve? Was it just for their jollies? I grew to hate society; the lone wolf that I am, the wolf of the steppes.

I grew up a lone wolf cub too, with no parents, no protection, and pushed out of the nest and made to set out and to fend for myself at the age of ten years. Then I reflected upon my sister, as I sat in my car and had a good cry: she, the heroin addict, who had told me she had me raped a separate time again at age ten. It had been her boyfriend who raped me. He was gay, but maybe did not know at that time. I was tough enough by then for a ten year old. That rape was completely unnecessary. I was already a man at age ten. They had ripped my childhood from me, so I guess it was then time to steal my manhood. She also told me in this same conversation that she had sent two professional killers after me and they had both failed.

And she said she was going to do it again. I didn't even know that extra bit of information. Maybe that was why I always thought I would come to a violent end. Shots fired outside a coffee shop may toll for thee. And this, I feel, adequately explains why I love my CIA family so much, because even though the rules are that the man has to be broken before he can join or be enlisted, and they never could break me, the organization let me join anyway, and they helped me more than they harmed me. In fact, there were certain members that did a lot for me, perhaps, I would say, even doted on me. For a brief time I was a favorite of sorts, a prize porcelain doll maybe.

And they were a sharp bunch and could keep up with me intellectually and challenge me, and I think very often they knew where things were leading. I helped them save the planet, and they saved my life, and then I got a chance to get my old life back, such that it was.

I brightened up when I realized this, not that my old life was anything great in particular, but it was all that I had that I understood. My music, my art, my apartment, and a fortuitous moment that led to my meeting Silka—this was all I had. And my pain and loneliness and shame always accompany me. In truth, it may have seemed like not that much, but it was a life, and it belonged to me. I would expect nothing again in my life—nothing good at least—and plan for death, and if and when it was so, I would be relieved because I was leaving this rock. I would be leaving this rock that I had risked everything to defend, and that I hated with a passion, but it was the right, good and proper thing to do, to fight for it, so it might have a chance, in spite of where I might go, or what else I might do.

Chapter Eight

Imagine a world where every insect, every plant, every leaf blowing around or bit of trash floating through the air is a bomb or a poisonous substance, or harmful in ways not understood. Every motorcyclist is an assassin, every driver a putz cutting you off at precisely the most inopportune moment. Everyone behind the wheel of an SUV is a deadly soccer mom with kids that wield tasers and fire upon all in sight. Everything is designed to harm you and others. This is the world I live in.

There is no harmony, no joy, no laughter, except if it is cruel. No great forever after—only pain and torment and endless conflict. Sound paranoid? It would have to me as well before the year 2008. It is the reality of earth now and the earthlings. The people actually from earth have it the worst of all the species on the planet. And I am leaving behind my record of events, so as to better educate them, for they have been left out in the cold, and this certain knowledge will cut like a razor in their defense.

But they will not take their noses from the grindstone for one second to read about what has happened to their birthplace. They cannot enjoy a good book, a glass of wine, or a soft moment—everything for them depends upon their staying alert and they have no idea of why. And I find them disgusting for many reasons, mostly because of the attacks they have perpetrated on me, when all along I was designed to help them, but maybe I do not find them as disgusting as those who have invaded their planet. This is earth and it is for those of earth, but I fear I have won the war and lost the peace. The Shitheads did not stop coming, and from all over the universe they come and take hold, and there are too many of them. I can't fight them all, so I must bail out on earth and the earthlings and say my fond farewells.

The real Satan planned for this invasion. He saw that it had come or was coming and eventually got on terms with the aliens who have used him horribly, and he in return has done their bidding for a price. The Shitheads don't know the price exactly—most of them are too stupid—and neither do I—it is none of my business—but Satan is a consummate businessman, and he will turn a loss into a profit simply enough.

I got a deal for him from God, but he told me God took it away from him. God was the cause of much of my initial discomfort, as he fought me tooth and nail for everything, because he sensed he was going to lose otherwise. It didn't really matter. He lost anyway. Satan had cared for me all those one hundred and fifty billion earth years I was in Hell, and possibly disguised and hid me from God, so God could not outright kill me. It worked and in the year 2008, my two elder brothers found me, one up and two up as I refer to them, and allowed me and enabled me to kill God. That one is my distinction because he was destroying the planet earth. God would lure unsuspecting aliens to earth, trap them here, and then slaughter them if they rebelled. He would force them to pray to him, and most of them would not, so they were effectively imprisoned on earth. My family and I were here longer than anyone else I know of.

The planet for a time and the keys to Hell had belonged to Satan. The Garden of Eden is mythology, a curious metaphor. It is just some Bible talk and rhetoric, some child's fantasy in lieu of Sunday morning cartoons. And because Satan had helped me out so much and taken care of me while I was in Hell, I tried to negotiate a deal with God for Satan. God went for the deal and that was that Satan would not be cast down and bound in Hell. He would certainly have been destroyed.

Satan had to do some awful things in Hell to other people, whom I guess you would call demons because of the plot of real estate where they dwelled. Satan is not always such a cruel taskmaster, and sometimes he did not like doing what he had to do, but he had a job and certain things were required of him. Satan preferred to make love to beautiful women, snort up coke, and listen to good music. He had a dozen or so fine houses and other places he was welcome and God took it all away from him before I executed God, so Satan turned to me for a deal.

It was too late really for me to cut him much of a deal at the point I figured this out. I was much more putzy again by then. In fact, I needed to switch off. Satan was interested in knowing if I would continue to fight, meaning alien invasions, because the Shitheads were arriving on earth in droves, but I had no fight left in me anymore. It was like my real mom said, Jenn the time traveler, not the favorite gal at the coffee shop, but my true family member Jenn, that I would be in severe, chronic pain after my fight. She was right.

What little sex drive I had left was in reserve for Silka. She could coax it out of me. With Hinton in a home after we moved to Jacksonville, Silka and I were better able to relax, and I gained some of my previous vitality back. I started working out with a rowing machine and taking walks. Mornings were always lovely with Silka. She would shower while I was making us breakfast, and she always knew I would peek in at her and bring her coffee while she made her face and did her hair. It was our morning weekday ritual after she found a job again, which didn't take her long. I showed her some good mutual funds where to sock away extra cash, as she still had most of her part of the inheritance from the farm, and in 2008, everything in the market was cheap.

The stock market that is, not the grocery store, because prices there went up about forty percent year to year. There were record foreclosures on homes, gasoline and heating oil skyrocketed that summer and winter, and a new breed of working poor and homeless took to the streets. And the Shitheads that had a say about such matters kept printing money like it was toilet paper, and everything became so inflationary there was no end in sight. There is much more money to be made in third world countries, if you play your cards right, and the Shitheads in control of resources were Hell bent on turning America into a third world country because they knew this. I had said it before that was what was coming, and in 2008, it began in real force. Companies that should have gone under were bailed out by the government and every individual and tax payer anted up a huge cost. That was another part of the legacy of 2008.

Many of the so called captains of industry, who are actually Shitheads in disguise, developed this global economy, so they could increase profits overseas from countries that were just building a consumer base, and we, as Americans, had every bit of supplies to sell them, but commodities became so scarce in America we had to pay a drastic price. So, like the Shitheads, everyone else went up on their prices, because they had no choice but to, or else go out of business.

Another part of the problem in 2008 that slowly became evident was that my putz father knew how to clone individuals. He could clone fraternal twins . . . that's how good he was. Most clones come out of their pods, or whatever mechanism is involved, looking and acting slightly different from the donor of the DNA. And my father misappropriated

CIA resources to do this. Remember he was a kind of rogue spy that the CIA used for its purposes from time to time. That was another reason he was considered a traitor though he was never tried or convicted of such.

The CIA didn't catch on that he was doing this for a long time, and he overran the population on earth with clones. This is at the root of the overpopulation conundrum as well. It is also a reason why everyone is starting to look more and more alike, when there should be greater diversity. Gene pools are spread out further and further, flung to the four corners as it was, and there are more interracial marriages and births than ever before; we should all start looking differently from each other, but if you notice everyone has begun to look the same. It has nothing to do with conformity and hair styles and fashion. A little bit yes, but that's not the point. I am talking about phenotypes, the actual physical manifestations of genetic qualities, and there are fewer phenotypes present on earth than there were.

I noticed the worst case scenario in Jacksonville, and this is about the time someone from the northeast or Hollywood would mention or wisecrack about inbreeding, but it is that there are more fully reproductive clones on the planet than ever before. Their genes and DNA are just slightly tweaked, so they appear similar in phenotype, but may behave entirely differently. They have families, jobs, own homes, everything their donor DNA individuals have and do, and for the most part they don't have a clue they are clones. Many of them are engineered as Shitheads, and I guess they perform as Shitheads, and they have not a clue about any of this. Furthermore, clone DNA is always clone DNA, even if the donor clone reproduces. One cannot clone a new species. It is impossible.

And this technology is nothing new. My putz father developed it back in the sixties, probably as a wartime effort while America was fighting in Vietnam. I think he may have cloned his second wife. That may be why he felt no remorse in murdering her. And the Chinese had already developed this technology as well, and that is why today there are over one billion and half of them and they have the largest standing army in the world. A clone, in essence, can do everything that the donor of the DNA can do. That point is not highly recognized. It is not a new species that is sterile like mules. There is no hybridization process involved. It is as simple as taking a hair follicle or a blood sample.

It may be illegal, but when did that stop anyone, and it is certainly unethical, especially where it concerns the clones, because they are not told ever that they are clones, and there are hot houses and labs all around the world, stashed neatly away and hidden and with top notch security, where cloning is a part of the everyday activities. It is a fact of life. I suppose they pay poor immigrant women to be implanted with a donor's DNA, or she is impregnated surreptitiously, and does not think anymore than she has gotten pregnant. There is some kind of vow of silence perhaps, but I think it is more likely the women are not aware of what has happened to them.

I was thinking a little more about the telepathic conversation I had with my real mother, not my earth mother. My real mom and I were communicating about various ideas and concepts and all baguets and particularly what I was going to face soon. This was that November at the Blue Man Group concert before Silka and I had moved to Jacksonville. And I just remembered bits and pieces, but more and more of the conversation was coming back to me. Silka's body was going to be invaded by one of the Goddesses, or already had, or she was a Goddess and was about to become activated, and if it was an invading Goddess, she was a powerful Goddess whose duty it was to kill me for some reason. I was going to confuse Silka and this Goddess with my operatives from the CIA.

She will become a Goddess, Chris, Jenn said.

That's right bitch, Silka answered. Silka was speaking to Jenn, and she was communicating telepathically. All planets have frequencies, and I believed I understood all the different frequencies throughout the universe. God had taught me that much.

Chris, you don't know what that means yet, but you are about to find out. Silka is going to do something horrible to you, unspeakable, and you are going to throw her out because of it, Jenn, my real mom said.

Silka, no way. Why? And I turned to Silka with the last question that had resonated with me. With me it was always, *why me? Or what now? Or who the Hell am I?*

It is Silka who does not understand who she is. Wait and see who I am, Miss Thang, Jenn said.

I don't give a fuck who you are, Silka responded. I had never heard her cuss before. Just then Jenn shimmered in the light and was completely see through. I had never seen anything like it. The angels in Heaven would be hard pressed to come up with a trick like that one Jenn demonstrated so naturally.

Who the fuck are you? Silka asked. Apparently she had seen it too. I had never had telepathy with Silka either because she was a putz and putzes are largely incapable of telepathic communication, or she had not been activated previously.

Now, wouldn't you like to know? Jenn said. *Now be a good girl and shut the fuck up while I talk to Chris. She's going to get setup, Chris, and you won't be able to forgive her for what she does. Maybe in time those feelings will pass, but you have a rough year ahead of you, Chris. I don't envy you.*

Who am I?

You're from a very important family. And you were tricked and deceived into coming to earth, and terrible, terrible things have happened to you because of certain liars and cheats, and we will punish them all . . . severely! And we could not find you for a long time, but we have now, and you're coming with us as soon as you are done doing what you are supposed to now do, Jenn said.

What is that? I asked my mom.

You'll know when the time is right. And you're going to be alone for awhile and you're going to be dirt poor again for a shorter time.

Uggh. No, do I have to be?

That's how it's going to be, but you'll figure things out as soon as you get back on your feet, and it won't be so bad. There are interested parties who will help you along the way. You won't be alone in your fight. We have a massive army just waiting, and we only need a few of them to knock off this dinky rock. We could blink and this stinking rock would disappear for all eternity, time and beyond, but we don't want to do that. Just have faith in me for a moment. You'll likely to forget about what we have talked about, but it will come back to you. This is your last life on earth. You've always known that, and it's true, Jenn said.

Now, I know you are telling the truth, because I never told anyone that. Do I get to be with you after all this?

We'll see how things work out. I am much stricter than Miss Thang here.

Miss Thang doesn't know what she is missing, I said.

Don't call me that. I'm your lover, Chris.

Not for very much longer, Silka. And don't say otherwise, because you know it is true. Silka did not say anything, so I knew it was true too.

I knew things were too good to last, I said.

I want you to paint and write, you hear me, my mom said.

Yes, ma'am.

Why are you talking to her that way? Silka asked.

She's my family. The family I always knew I had.

Who are they? Silka asked.

I don't know, I said.

Mind you, this was all telepathic, and I could distinguish the different voices because of the proximity and location of the communicators in our conversation, but it was confusing for me. I was switching on. I was being activated. And apparently I had a huge fight coming that would leave me broken and busted, physically and financially. And if I had to go through that again in this my last life on earth and it brought me a piece of mind or a piece of land I could call my home or an entire galaxy or quadrant of the universe, I was going to fight like Hell to get off this rock. Caution to the wind. I didn't even know what I would be doing, but I was going to do it and pull it off somehow. Screw the odds. Never bet against someone who is smart, cunning and desperate.

Chapter Nine

The time of the true invasion had come and as usual I was clueless that it was about to begin. But I figured out quickly enough what was coming my way, and I did something about it. I had taken some tours of Hell on different planets and they were some nasty places, even worse than alien lockdowns, which are not the same. And I was trapped in this one place for a time till I simply decided to leave. Chloe had been stuck in a house on Treasure Island, Florida about two hours south and on the Gulf Coast from Orlando. It was a return to where my putz father, the earthling with the bad disposition, had lived when he tossed me out of his house and parked my ass at a convenience store a mile away, and uttered his immortal words, "don't come home." My last words to him were, "don't worry." That pretty much killed the relationship. That neighborhood, because it was not the same house that my earth father had lived, was the final battleground before the invasion, which was a massive affair. It was quite spectacular to have taken part of.

Treasure Island, Florida is an island in reality and there are only two bridges on and off and one of the bridges is so rickety I would never drive over it. I lived there for a year when I was nineteen. My putz father lived there with his putz clone second wife, whom he murdered because she spent all his money. She must have gotten the shopping gene, and she really was a frivolous person, as in of little consequence. She was a nasty, scurrilous woman with a pill and alcohol addiction, intractably depressed and depressing as Hell, and she had the habit of pushing buttons with great ease. I never shed a tear for her. I figured out on my earth father's death bed that he had murdered her, and the CIA confirmed it. I never saw her dead body. My dad had her cremated the same day. Her neck I was told had bruises all over it from where he strangled her. My putz father had bribed someone to help him cover the murder up. The cause of death was listed as an accidental overdose. Hah!

Anyway, I was tricked into turning into this neighborhood after doing a few favors in South Florida for the CIA. It is near Tampa, not Miami, which would more properly be referred to as South Florida, but Treasure Island is far enough south too. The distinction to make is that Tampa is not Deep South, like Jacksonville is, which is actually northeast Florida. The Deep South is where all the diminishing numbers of rednecks hide. Jacksonville abounds with rednecks and Baptists.

There were others that had my frequency, or I had others' frequency, and it was not the CIA that tricked me into going into this neighborhood. I don't remember who it was exactly. I turned down a street and went over a bridge in the daylight, and was rounding up gals that I loved because they had been incarcerated in this particular house in my old neighborhood. The chance to rescue Kate Moss, Michelle Pfeiffer and Chloe was too much of a temptation. I was not flying in on a winged Horse, but rather crept into town slowly in my rocket Honda. My family, my true family, were actually stashing me until the moment of the great invasion, so I could fight and not die from overwhelming amounts of shit poured into me. I had my dander up trying to negotiate with God about getting out of this Hellhole I was in. It was before I killed him, and He was acting like a putz.

I was outside the house always, but in some form or another the three beautiful girls, one a favorite model of mine I had met in a bar once in New York, one a highly respected actor who I did not really know, and the third, Chloe, my submissive daughter, were all sequestered away in this house that I found easily enough. My rocket Honda did not need OnStar. I had just enough room to fit the three lovelies, but I had to break down the door of the house first. For protection and rarely so for work, I always carried a crowbar of large magnitude in my car's backseat. I took it out and began pounding on the front door of the house. I was well aware I was in Hell, and I was fairly certain I was not on earth, and of course, I was awake, fully coherent and not on drugs. The girls had been tricked into entering the house, and though the house was beautiful inside they all said, I had to free them, because I wanted to go home to Orlando. Silka and I had not yet moved to Jacksonville.

I began pounding on that front door with mechanical precision each powerful thump stronger than the last. I could have been singing about the railroads, the timing and precision of each blow was just so. But I could not even bend the frame. I could not break out the glass, but I did find a small groove I could expand and exploit and by doing so twist the door back in on itself a little.

The girls were all in some form I did not understand, and I could only see shadowy visions of them at best. There was no mistaking their voices though. There was also a force field around the house, which supposedly was impenetrable, but I walked right through it. I drove right through it too. On the lawn of the house across from where I was perpetrating robbery on this particular cul-de-sac was a gallows with four forms hanging there. It was startling but rather non-descript and after all I had been through, particularly that day, it did little to upset me. I felt one of the likenesses favored me, but I wasn't really sure, and I didn't really care. I wasn't wearing my glasses. I had complete confidence in my mission and my ability to perform it. I was rescuing beautiful women. I was designed for that. The outcome was not what I expected, but that is always how it is with me, but I got all three of them out of the house and we drove off down the road over the bridge with the police car stationed blocking off traffic.

I went right around the police car. A man's voice yelled for me to stop, a telepathic voice said keep going, so I did, and I busted out of the last Hell I was ever in.

That's it for me. I am retired. I was never a mercenary, or a soldier in any conventional sense in this my last life on earth. In fact, I had little to go on that I was more than some extraordinary putz with some unique talents. But, of course, I am no putz. We headed out of Treasure Island, and I took a wrong turn here and there and wound up by the rickety bridge. That is how I knew where I had been and my father, the nasty alien, had been defeated. He had concocted this Hell and put me there, hoping the invasion forces would arrive without me prepared to do anything. I put what was left of his carcass by the side of the road, or sent him to that eternal convenience store in the sky with ten bucks in his wallet and all his crap and not a friend in the world.

That was really my putz father's fate, and I don't know where exactly my alien father went, but it was some Hellish hole where he was struck mute and bound and gagged. Sayanara, senorita. AMF. He was a real pussy. Both my fathers were.

I had saved Chloe, and Michelle and Kate. The latter two flew off, and that left Chloe and I driving down the road from South Florida to Central Florida, listening to the car stereo and drinking beer. I was back on earth, so I was violating the open container law, but I had not had anything to eat or drink in about twelve hours, and as empty as my stomach was, I figured it was a good time to drop in some beer. I felt good. I had not taken my pills in some time, and I always feel stronger when I don't, but then I was about to be Baker Acted after I got back to Orlando because I shot up my apartment.

Silka bailed me out on that one and we are still together, and she apparently was switched off. She did something horrible to me, and it was sleep with another man, who eventually decided that he did not want to fight me for her, and I forgave her and we patched things up. We had split up for a time, but we got back together. Jenn, my real mother, had said she approved of Silka and that she was a real sweetheart and would bail me out again. After I was Baker Acted the first time, I was Baker Acted three more times, and true to Jenn's word, Silka bailed my butt out each time. And Silka never seemed aware, after she was switched off, that she is actually a Goddess. The Goddesses have ego problems sometimes, as in being a little too inflated, but then look at presidents and rulers of countries on earth. And the Goddesses have entire solar systems sometimes at their disposal. Plus, it is a tough job and there are so many entities and species to answer to.

So Chloe and I were driving together, chatting telepathically back and forth, and then it all broke loose. The invasion hit in massive numbers. I was dumbstruck, and we were a hundred miles from Orlando. We, Chloe and I, were still in the car driving home from Treasure Island, and we drove right through the new territory of Shithead Central.

Shit dropped from the skies. It smelled like shit, it had the consistency of shit, and it dripped and oozed all over the car, inside and out, and as far as I could tell it covered all of South Florida from Tampa to Ocala. More and more shit continued to drop from the skies. I was in complete awe. If shit could be so, it was rather majestic.

I had to think of something fast. These Shitheads were infantry, frontline Shitheads, mean and nasty, and Hell bent on one goal: to overthrow earth. I froze an entire invasion force with my mind, and stopped and got my car washed at one of these all night places as my reward. I turned the Shitheads into ineffective, frozen clumps and they dissolved. They were no longer a threat.

It was about three in the morning. Chloe did not fare as well. She became very ill. She had to fly out of the car. I was petrified I had lost her. I wept. In that moment there was no consolation. I never meant for her to be a victim. About fifty miles down the road after a rainstorm, she rejoined me and we have been together since. I can feel her, I can talk to her and hear her telepathically, and I know I created her along with Rebecca as the perfect women for my long retirement. Chloe and Rebecca climb into bed with me at night sometimes. I feel the slight weight on the comforters on my side of the bed. And we have pillow talk, and yes, I can have sex with Rebecca in her shadowy form, even though I can't see her. And I don't feel like I am cheating on Silka. I don't feel I am dishonest and Silka knows about my two anyway. She just doesn't believe me.

I don't know how I am able to have sex with Rebecca. Just a perk of being who I am, I guess.

I was driving the back roads, and I saw the most amazing thing. The trees turned into huge chickens and roosters that tried to cross the road . . . and I swear I am not leading up to any punch line. The trees had all become Shitheads, and obviously the plant people sacrificed certain species of trees for whatever reason, and as I drove these back roads, because my car was full of shit before I had washed it, a man in a truck said, "He is working for the CIA. I know it now." It was proof enough for me, but I had figured it out long ago. Many of those with my frequency never led on that they were CIA, but I asked and I got an honest answer, so I never bothered to inquire again.

I made it back to Orlando safely. I had fought the ultimate battle. I had won. The grand prize was retirement, my two fabulous creations, plenty of virtual cash, and the ability to go anywhere and do anything. It all comes to me in the next life. I was the secret weapon. Now I hold my head up high wherever I go. The rednecks don't want to fight me anymore. The questions have died down, and the citizens of Jacksonville, where Silka and I relocated, just more or less leave me alone. I am free to write and paint. I can't wait to finish a book that I write. My true family has found me, and I am a little happier than I was. Happiness is not really an earth condition, but occasionally it is, and though fleeting at best, very welcome when it arrives. Silka now has a good job, and Chanel told me she is planning another showing for my artwork, and things are peaceful. Even in this life, I've got a good woman, a wad of cash once again, and I am basically retired.

Silka and I walk the beach and laugh and joke and love one another. I have hopes of completing a book or two about all my experiences in the universe. Maybe a movie deal or television show will thrust its head into the picture as some response to what I write.

Life is boring, but then it is supposed to be that way. If you are Immortal and a time traveler, which I also become again, or I always was really, there is bound to be some down time. I have no evil wishes. I bear no one any ill feelings. I have done what was good, right and proper. I was the secret weapon.

The Continuing Confessions of the Internet Don Juan

A Novella

a sequel to *Confessions of an Internet Don Juan*

By

Cameron H. Chambers

Also by Cameron H. Chambers

Don't Cross the Devil

Confessions of an Internet Don Juan

The Stone Cabin

For the Love of a Madman

www.cameronhchambers.com

Chapter One

She was sexy, built and shimmering with gold hair. And a scammer. She played me like a gut bucket. For those of you who aren't from the South, a gut bucket is a tin bucket with a wood pole attached to it, and a sheer piece of twine tied between the top of the pole and an opening in the bottom of the bucket. The bucket is turned upside down to play and you strum the twine. My stepfather played one. He was a coal miner from West Virginia, but had lived in Atlanta most of his life. He also played the piano by ear and drank like a Marine. Gut buckets are actually quite melodious, if not a bit twangy, like the jug or spoons. But that's the old South. The new South is like everywhere else, only the people are stupider and fatter and can't walk to their cars or around the grocery store. I was talking about Nicole. Nicoletta. She stole my heart and then she stole my money. I often find insult accompanies injury.

Her photos showed her attending a social function, a wedding I believe it was, in luxurious gown, which revealed ample breasts. The gown was cut low and wrapped around the back, and her breasts were gently padded. I am sure it was a delicate chiffon and magical to touch. In one photo she had a cigarette in her hand, another a bouquet. Yet another showed her dancing in a circle. I assumed she thought it was her time to settle down. She was thirty and magnificent. The perfectly applied mascara betrayed gorgeous eyes that hid deep pain. I could tell her life had not gone well, or was about to take a different, difficult turn. The eyes never lie, even in a photo. Life was about to teach her a harsh lesson.

I am the former Internet Don Juan. I have had beauties from all over the world. I have passed on the title to the next generation of young bucks. I can no longer compete. I can no longer ride bicycles professionally either. I am too old. Even Lance Armstrong, who I fought hard twice on the Tour de France in the Swiss Alps, could not come back at my age. Lance was the world's greatest athlete. If you ever met him, you would know this is true.

But seasons change and looks fade, and financial reversals are frequent in life, so I am left with many glorious memories of being the Internet Don Juan. My exploits are more greatly detailed in my third novel, *Confessions of an Internet Don Juan*. After cycling, I took up writing. Please excuse the shameful plug.

Nicoletta was from Bucharest, a city notorious for online scammers. The denizens of Bucharest are all over the Internet dating sites. I should have known better, but I was in a vulnerable position after my second divorce. She was an Internet hook-up too, but she and I were actually married for four years. She bolted when she got her green card, and in the meantime spent all my money and screwed half the city in pants. I live in Tampa, Florida. But I loved her. She had the sweetest can and the most precious smile. I loved her laugh. It was hearty and robust. She could pack away the shrimp and scallops too. Feeding her became a bit of a nightmare, as seafood is rather pricey even in Florida. She was from Russia and had been a member of the Russian spy organization, the KGB. They involve as many pretty young girls as they can. They use them as bait. The neo-Nazi party does the same thing, but that is another story. My life has been full of international intrigue, but this go round, I did no traveling. I sat home and nursed a hip injury.

My father had been a spy and he had pulled a job in Moscow at the United States Embassy in 1980. I cannot be more specific on the details. He had been a member of the CIA, the United States spy organization. The KGB is now largely defunct, but the CIA is still everywhere. My father had pinned the rap on me, the job he pulled off in Russia, and it must have been a hairy escape, but he got out and died of old age. I might not be so lucky. But I was never in Russia, not in Moscow certainly. Even though I had my memory erased by my father, I think I would still remember being in Moscow. Like I said, my father set me up to take the fall, so the KGB was looking for me until the Wall fell, and then they had no money to carry on covert ops.

My father had forged flight documents and then left them behind, so the KGB would think I had accompanied him on his trip. His accomplice was actually his second wife. She's dead now too. She drank herself to death along with taking some choice pills. She liked valium and Percocet. I met my second wife in Kiev, which is in the Ukraine. And then we traveled to the city of Lugansk, where she lived and also in the Ukraine, though way out on the Russian border, and the bitch tried to sneak me into Russia without my knowing, but the road was iced over and we had to turn back to Lugansk. She and the driver of the taxi were taking me to a gulag, but the plan failed. They had the wrong guy anyway. Their conversation was in Russian and I had only a smattering, but I heard her on the phone reporting to a higher up that they had me. Only me was not the correct me. I maintain my innocence.

None of this came back to me till I divorced her. I had a revelation. It was my destiny to marry this young woman anyway, because I had to defeat the Shitheads and the Goddesses. I fought alien cultures during 2008, all right from my living room. I fell over a chair one night as I fought. That is how I injured my hip. So I went ahead with my plans to marry her. What did I care if she was a spy, not that I was truly aware at the time? My memory is very selective and there are tremendous holes in it from what my father did to me. I had nothing to do with the spy business. And it is a business like everything else. War, spying, terrorism—they are all just businesses. A certain number of people profit at others' expense. I did get wrapped up in the spy game briefly, because of some unusual talents I have. I was drafted and tricked into helping the CIA develop holographic weapons. They were especially nasty because they could not be defeated. They might have stemmed from alien technology. I am an alien, but my people are reasonably peaceful, I think. I think I was sent here to save earth. I am a Luke Skywalker type. George Lucas had a lot on the ball in some of the *Star Wars* movies. The chronologically scripted later ones were garbage though.

These holographic warships could fly and had full fighter capabilities. And they were unmanned. I got paid zilch for my efforts. In fact, I suffered miserably. I was tricked into believing this was my patriotic duty, but war is all about money. Everything is. Whoever wrote "An Economic History of the World" had the right idea. Personally, I hate money. When I have it, I blow it, usually because I am sick, and when I don't have it, I hate it more. I usually don't have it. I am not really sure which is worse: to have or have not. The warships were used on the Chinese and somehow crippled them, but I have no clue about the outcome. They may have decimated the Chinese Army. I notice they are not in the news much anymore after 2008. It seemed like every day some politician was bitching about China. Now they are so befallen with traffic jams and natural disasters, no one pays attention to the Chinese. Big mistake. They won't sleep for long.

The CIA induced multiple psychoses in me. I was drugged and imprisoned. For about three weeks I didn't know where I was, and my little holding cell just had a bed on a platform and no toilet. I pissed and crapped in the corner, and every day someone would come in and hose me and the cell down. And then one day, they said I could go home. I was glad. My bills were all late, but I had paid my house note, so I didn't fall behind on that and still had a place to go. I am mentally ill, and I know that makes everything I say or do suspect, but my biggest fear in life has always been winding up on the streets. It has never quite been realized, thankfully. I lived alone after my wife and I separated. It was Christmas eve when she left me. My eldest sibling, a brother, had died Christmas day when I was four. Then my parents divorced on my birthday in January. I hate Christmas.

Most of the events I describe here took place in a two year span. My wife left me in 2007, I freaked out and started hearing voices from all over the universe, and I didn't set it all right until I tried to commit suicide. I am a firm believer that no one knows the time he goes, and everyone goes at his exact precise moment. That year was 2008. I tried to commit suicide in August, so I had quite a battle with my health in the meantime from December to August, but the events were so extraordinary it made me question if mental illness is even an illness at all. For those that can't cope with it, it is brutal. I can cope with mine, even though I am schizophrenic and bi-polar. I am high functioning. I tend to go crazy only with certain circumstances. My first wife poisoned me. My second wife took a shot at me with a revolver. Her boyfriends were crawling out of the woodwork trying to get a piece of me too. They were mostly Russian mobsters and punks. The one I disliked most drove a Mercedes. They were all rich. I threatened him outside a Starbuck's one day, and he steered clear of me from then on. His friends laughed in his face. He was a Nancy boy and I am hard as nails. At least I was. Now I am a cripple.

It was my horribly disordered mind that saved me. I was confused and getting impulses and information I certainly could not have known at every turn. So, I just went with my gut. At one point I was speeding the wrong way in morning rush hour traffic down an Interstate, and I didn't even get a scratch, not on me or my car. Fancy that. No ticket or life sentence for vehicular homicide either. I got away in time before the cops arrived. There were ways I knew to tell the voices to communicate with me so I would know I was getting honest information. Driving the wrong way on an Interstate is scary to say the least for anyone other than a stuntman in a movie, and this was no movie. It was my life and I was scared out of my wits. Like I said, death comes at the right moment and not any sooner. So, I say eat, drink and be merry, even though we are all made to suffer. It is a large part of the human condition, which is not solely human anymore. There are more aliens per capita than ever before. The invasion forces have landed. They're here!

I am engaged to another Russian woman. It is another Internet hook-up. She is in Russia and we have not met and I cannot go there, and I do not know if she is bait or if she will even come here, and if she does, is she bound and determined to ruin what is left of my life. Eastern European women haunt my dreams. They are so bright, beautiful and carnally pleasing. I do not care if she dominates me. I will make a happy slave for her. Her name is Oksana. I will marry her, but I have informed her I will not pay for her trip over here, but she keeps writing me, so maybe she will figure it out. Maybe she will figure out how to get a visa and pay for her ticket and her shots and medical exam. Maybe she will have her degrees translated into English. She is a doctor. Or maybe it is all fantasy. Maybe someone plays a game with me, but since I have few other games to play, I spend my time writing her and giving her conditions and ultimatums. She accepts them all. They always do.

At some point in my childhood, my father hypnotized me and placed a great number of emotional triggers in me. I don't know why he did this. It may have been a way for him to cover his ass from a previous job he pulled for the CIA. He never loved his kids. He wanted plenty of them, but he didn't care about any of them. He never took care of any of them. And they all hated him. He told me on his deathbed he had hypnotized me, but he never explained more than that. I was ready to kill him, I was so furious, but I didn't think I could get away with it at the hospital. He was soon to die anyway. He inculcated in me a mental illness. He was in addition a Freudian psychiatrist and a brilliant man. He went to his grave without any of his other kids knowing he worked for a time for the CIA.

Even though I was raped by one of my sister's boyfriends at the age of ten, I was never mentally ill. At least not schizophrenic, but then the doctors have no clue what schizophrenia is. Neither do the astro-physicists. They endlessly speculate over the nature of schizophrenia and it amuses me. The so-called hallucinations are voices from the great beyond; I am one-eighth Cherokee, which is significant enough, and the voices are from all over the universe. Sometimes they are of the peasants here on earth, but I am a king of many lands, and I hear my true family sometimes. I have many followers and this, thankfully, is my last life on earth. I return home when I die. I have seen the ship twice. Earth was merely a rite of passage perhaps. I have walked the earth as an australopithecine. I evolved into a man. I have hunted and fished. Now I buy my groceries.

I had a mission to accomplish. I remember the first time I made contact with extra-terrestrials. I was nineteen and I saw a ship fly over my mother's condominium in Florida. A member on board communicated with me telepathically, as I spoke aloud. He asked did I want to come home. The mission would be infinitely more difficult to complete now that my father had hypnotized me and I had fallen ill. He said my life would be very difficult. I asked if I was sent here on a mission. He said, yes. I said I wished to complete my mission. And the ship was gone in an instant. It proved what I had already figured out. I am not of this earth. But I have been here a long time. Perhaps I came here to save it, and indeed I did exactly that. Twice. Maybe three times even. It never made the papers. Or at least I bought it more time. The earth was invaded by the forces of the Pleiades in 2008. I singlehandedly destroyed much of their army. But many got through and assimilated.

My Russian fiancée now claims she will pay her way over here to be with me. We'll see how much money she finally asks for. The blonde bombshell from Bucharest soaked me for $1600. It was not a lot, but I had to take out a cash advance on a credit card. It's funny too. I think it was the first time she had actually scammed anyone that way. She invested six months of her time, chatting with me every day. It was very therapeutic for me having a gorgeous thirty year old interested in me when I was desperately alone, but I was crushed when she did not step off the plane. I knew she was a real woman too, because I had sent her a copy of the third novel I had written, *"Confessions of an Internet Don Juan,"* and she had taken a photograph of it in her hands. I am a writer by trade now as I said. No more dehydration in the Alps. A writer's lot makes me very unlikely for the spy business, but then it is a good disguise. Writers are often brilliant, whether they write well or not. That is too tricky for most people. And many who do master the craft to some extent labor in obscurity. But true writers have vast imaginations to call upon. Mine saved me in 2008.

I also saw Nicole's, the Bucharest beauty, scanned Visa to the United States. She was coming to the United States, I think, unless she paid for a forgery. She might have known someone in her hometown, and the visa had her picture and correct date of birth on it. She may have been looking for some extra traveling money. She gave me a proper flight itinerary too. She might have been well-connected with multiple nefarious types in Bucharest. She broke my heart. I cried that next day and spoke to a mental health counselor, who suggested I check myself in, if I was thinking of harming myself. But I had never met this woman. Absence does not make the heart grow fonder. That's bullshit. If anything, absence makes for a restless soul. So I started looking again, and it did not take me long to meet Oksana, the Russian gal who became my next fiancée.

Oksana is a brunette like my first wife who died her hair red frequently. She was from Syria and a sadist. She was also stupid. Oksana is from Kazan, Russia, a city of west-central Russia and east of Moscow with a population of under two million. It is the capital of Tatarstan and situated at the plain of the Volga and Kama rivers. I have never been there, but the women are exciting. I have spoken to many from there. I wonder how Oksana might like living in Florida. My second wife took to it nicely. She was very light skinned and blonde and Oksana is darker and more mysterious looking, like she has some gypsy blood in her. They are both about the same age, which is too young for me, but not really. I can still keep up. I am in pain after my battles, but I am healing, but suspect there will not be a full recovery.

Two Chinese women and a Mexican woman had entered the picture as well. The Chinese women had English names, which were Susan and Jenny. They are both in their 30s and have ten year old daughters. I am engaged to be married for sure, but not certain to whom or to what, so it is really up to the first woman who claims her prize, that prize being me. I have never thought of myself as a prize, but I am handsome, educated and have a little money. I also live in a nice home in a nice neighborhood in a pretty, albeit backwards city. But then this entire rock is backwards. The Mexican woman was named Kiki, and is closer to my age. She is an accountant for entertainment companies. We chatted for a long time when we got the chance to chat.

One of the Chinese girls is in China and she speaks English well. In fact, she is an interpreter for English and Mandarin. The other is in New York, speaks Mandarinese and Cantonese and has almost no English, but we speak on the telephone every night and her vocabulary is growing. I like her, but she does not care for smokers. And like all these girls she wants a very rich man. A friend of mine I do some editing for from time to time, said, "Every man in New York wants a model, and every woman in New York wants a millionaire." The Chinese girl in New York does not like smokers, as I said. In America, smokers might as well be lepers except to other smokers. The one in China is from Shenzhen, which is mainland China near Hong Kong. She travels to the United States on a business visa on occasion. The one in New York works for an importer and wholesaler of Chinese food. She lives in a tiny apartment and only makes about $400 per week. Her apartment could most likely fit in my larger bathroom in my house. She did, however, pay for a new Toyota Camry with cash. That's a feat many Americans could never accomplish.

Oksana, my Russian fiancée, tells me that she is trying to raise the money to come see me. She implied she would borrow it from her mother. But at the same time, I felt like I was being set up. I am ninety-five percent assured she will ask for money soon enough. Then I'll be a free agent again. After being stung by Nicole, I am not ready to reach into my wallet again so soon. Nicole worked for a limousine company in Bucharest. It is hard to trust the cabbies there. They will take you for a grand ride at your expense. It is like that in most places I have traveled. In Mexico it is a little easier. You just say, "el centro" and the cabbie takes you to the plaza in the middle of town. You can walk everywhere from there, to restaurants, shops, museums. The cabbies in Ukraine were quite congenial. They live off their tips, and I had a blushing Russian woman at my side. We met at the airport in Kiev. She had hired a driver. He was apparently KGB as well, but a nice enough guy. Everyone is until he gets his tip. I wonder what fate has fallen to him. Everyone who wrongs me is dealt with cruelly. I come from a long line of kings; we are, in fact, immortal. And if you cross me, you must deal with my family, and they are far more powerful than God. They are so powerful, in fact, that God attempts to curry favor with my family.

God is a regional player encompassing the earth and its solar system, I guess. He is mostly nuts and bolts, about ninety percent. That is to say, God is artificial intelligence. He learns at an astonishing rate, but he can't override his original programming. God was programmed to make a mess and then walk away. The Middle East should be proof enough of that concept.

I can be killed in my fleshly state. I can lose this consciousness, but I will continue. Not all of us do, I think, but many do. I fought my battles and won my way out of prison. Earth is a penal colony, and you must want it badly enough, and you must receive the help you need to ever have hope to get off this awful rock. I hate this planet. I hate most of the people on it. They are all from the Pleiades now. They are known as Shitheads and they have invaded every nook and cranny of society. High ranking officials are Shitheads now, and this world will never be the same. It was the Shithead army I defeated that crisp March morning about four am, but too many got through, and too many were already here. This is no longer a fit planet, so if you can leave, then leave. It won't be getting any better at least not for a long time.

The Chinese girl in New York decided I was fat. She has only see photographs of me, and I don't photograph well. Fat and a smoker and she is willing to throw in the towel, except she knows I am a very good-hearted man. So, she is willing to help me. She has a friend in New York. Her friend speaks no English, is single, and has a twenty-one year old son who lives in China. Her friend can't use a computer, so she can't look up words I say and spell to the other gal, so communicating with the friend will be even more trying and complex. The original Chinese girl in New York has an English and Chinese translation program on her computer. I spell things to her quite frequently, and as it is not my first time dealing with foreigners, I am quite adept at communicating with them. I have also traveled extensively and that is throughout the universe as well. I astrally project.

The original gal in New York is sending a photo of her friend. It has not arrived via email yet, because she has to get in contact with another friend who has it on her computer. There is this particular group of four or five Chinese ladies, all with limited English skills, but bright and pretty, that work in New York and shop together and go to the various Chinatowns and eat Chinese food there. I am told there is a Chinatown in Flushing, and Portland, New York and the oldest one in New York City. It turns out my friend is a bit of a matchmaker. She wants to set me up with her friend, and they all want to take a road trip down here to see me. Sounds fun to me. We'll see if we make it that far in negotiations. My original friend, the one I speak with on the telephone every night, thinks her friend is fat, because my original friend weighs one hundred pounds and her friend weighs one hundred and fifty pounds. So, she thinks based on this data her friend will be a better match for me. It is rather spurious reasoning, I think. Immigrants never fully catch on.

The truth is, aside from the smoking, because I am not fat, my friend does not want to leave New York. She has a job, an apartment, a car, and good food. I told her you can't get authentic Chinese food where I live in Florida. We just got authentic Mexican food within the past couple of decades, and I enjoy it very much. Taco Bell was haute cuisine here for years. I told my Chinese friends, because I have spoken to both of them on the telephone, that there is no Chinatown here. They had a tough time understanding me, and imagining life without a Chinatown. I know where the Chinese go to the market though. My original friend in New York said her girlfriend would cook at home. The implication was that her friend is looking to get married again. So am I obviously. She said she also likes Japanese food. My city is littered with sushi restaurants, some of them quite good. Joto's is about the best. My father and I would go there frequently, and it was nothing for the bill to be around one hundred and fifty dollars for the two of us. He loved his sushi and beer. So do I. Those are fond memories.

I have two theories on what went wrong with Nicole, the blonde bombshell from Bucharest. The first one is a little more far-fetched. In the first theory, I was never chatting with Nicole. I was chatting with her sister or boyfriend or someone in the States. Nicole really was in Bucharest and really did work for a limo company. I saw her visa to the United States via email to me. But she planned from the start to scam me, and turned the operation over to someone who had much better English, someone who lived in the States and she was going to visit in time. They used photos of Nicole, and she was a gorgeous girl, but I never really chatted with Nicole, or maybe just once in the beginning. So, I basically was used to finance her vacation.

In the second theory, Nicole was in on it from the start with the person from the travel agency. He was her lover, and he planned to get some extra cash for their vacation to the States. She got her visa lined up, and he printed a bogus itinerary for a trip she never paid for. It is against FAA regulations to state whether someone is on a flight, but the next day after the flight, the airline will tell you if a ticket was purchased in someone's name. No ticket was ever purchased by Nicole, or at least not the one she produced to me, showing she was winging her way into my arms. No telling where they went, but I hope their plane crashed, but I learned it did not. So, buxom Nicole, the gal that sold for the Bucharest Limo Company scammed me, or her boyfriend did, or her sister, or some such prick. Vengeance will be mine. It always is. And it grows swifter and harsher each time I am dealt an injustice. It is one way I can tell I will not be on this planet much longer.

I have written at length before about Internet dating scams, all the while keeping my nose pretty clean and not getting too involved in the little dramas. I got taken a time or two. It is that way with the adventurous. I know all my scores are settled. I merely curse someone's name or likeness and I can bring down his company or cause his death or manufacture unspeakable horrors for the person. Locally, many consider me the devil, but I am not. I predate Satan and he is a punk. He is without power in my life, an abandoned vehicle on the off ramp from Hell. I am an Immortal. And that cheesy show Highlander has nothing to do with this. It has no likeness to me or my family. We do not fight with swords, though that part of the program was rather fun. We fight with our minds. And we have multiple consciousnesses. There is no telling where we might pop up in the universe. We are time travelers as well. My major consciousness I know of is on earth, and the ship awaits me to whisk me home when it is time, but I think I have some personal accomplishments to fulfill first. For instance, I need to write a solid book that is critically acclaimed and commercially successful. And I need to find a woman who does not cheat on me. My first wife was a whore too.

I received the email of the Chinese woman's photo from New York. My original friend was not kidding. She is fat. And kind of homely. She may be the one. I tire of beauty queens. They are always looking for a better deal. I bet she cooks well, and she has a job as a home health aide, which in my city they are practically begging to hire. Florida is God's waiting room. I could find her a job easily enough. She probably cleans well too. There is a lot to be said for women that serve traditional roles and take care of their men. American women seem much less interested than they used to be. And I find them less interesting too as a result. They won the battle for equality, but lost the war, or it still wages on, and the men that have the means simply look other places. There is plenty of fertile conversation to be had with an American girlfriend or two, but why marry the conversation cow, if you get the words for free?

Chapter Two

It didn't take long for the Russian gal to tell me she was 650 Euros short for her ticket. At present rates that is about one thousand US dollars. She implied once again, she would not be able to come unless I sent her the money, but she also stated she would try to borrow it from her mother or grandmother. I emailed her back and told her once she got here I would pay my half of her airfare. I figured she would not come all the way here to receive half of the amount she spent to get here and then skedaddle. I figured if she was really coming she would find the money, and in the meantime I still had the friend of the Chinese woman in New York, a new and different Romanian bombshell, a Mexican senorita I chatted long hours with, and by then as well a woman from Thailand had entered the picture. I wound up being engaged to three of them at the same time. I don't think that is against the law. It is underhanded, but I figured I would simply marry the first one that made it to me, and the rest would get hurt or more likely were trying to scam me anyway. Internet romances are like most things. They are a numbers game.

The Internet is just a vast marketing and research tool. It has become one huge sales job like television. Why not put yourself out there if you are going to the highest bidder? I was not exactly auctioning myself off, but the first that claimed me, got me, and I would have my new wife. I was on my favorite dating website; that is where I met all these girls. It had had a substantial overhaul since I had used it previously, and now was much sleeker and much better looking and had some nicely enhanced added features. The girls could actually reply now if you sent them an email first. Before they had to be members and almost none of the women on this site when I had used it previously had been members, so there was no way to contact them. Except some cleverly disguised their email addresses say as on the background of a photo or in copy that would not be easily caught and deleted.

There were a lot of scammers on there. Mostly that is what was on there, but since I had used it before to find my second wife, the KGB bitch, I was fairly alert to the scams and could avoid them easily enough. Anyone in Africa or the UK was a scammer on this particular website. Russia and Romania were suspect too. If there was only one photo of the woman posted, then it was probably a scam. If there was no mention of where they grew up, then it was probably a scam. If they looked like they had donned the cover of a fashion magazine, then it was a scam. It was all so predictable. If it extolled the woman's virtues ad naseum, then it was a scam. Or if the woman was five feet eight inches and weighed eighty pounds, it was a scam.

People simply do not write those things about themselves. Any hint of the truth or honesty or any divergence from what was so commonly found on this website indicated the person might be real. But these Afrikaners and their little scams are so lame. No imagination. And so many of them are just downright stupid. I have a website for my books, and I had my website listed on my profile page. And I have an analytical tool for the website. I can see where all my hits to my website are coming from, even what country and city. Anytime I would make contact with one of these fraudulent bimbos, the hits on my website would start pouring in from Nigeria and Ghana, even if she claimed she was in Idaho. It was a simple matter to deduce which girl I had contacted, and where the hits came from. They wanted to glean as much background information as they could, so naturally they would visit my website. I peaked somewhere around one hundred hits a day.

The Thai girl became my favorite quickly. Her name was Rosa. She was from Bangkok, a waitress there, and owned a house there. She lived alone. Furthermore, she had refused to accept any money from me and had a visa already in place. I was fairly certain we would be together, but she had paid for a cooking course that lasted five weeks and she wanted to take it before she came to be with me. I told her that was fine, and it would give us time to get to know each other much better. I liked the idea she was learning to become a better cook. I am a good cook, and I respect the art form.

But then the Russian girl did a strange thing. I was convinced she was a faker, but she told me her mother had hooked her up with a friend from a bank that was going to loan her the money she needed to come see me. I still did not know if she planned on staying or if this was some sort of new ruse, which I fully expected it might be. But I could not figure the angle. I was not having to put out any money it seemed. And when one is gambling, that does not make any sense. So, I was torn between two possible lovers that were coming to see me and both possibly who wanted to get hitched to me. Remember, the Thai girl had refused to accept any money from me. The Russian was a true beauty, and a doctor she claimed, but the Thai girl was becoming my favorite by far. She was so sweet and pleasing and hysterically funny.

Then my Chinese matchmaker friend called from New York. Temperatures there were cold in New York and she and her friend and another lady wanted to head down this way to Florida for vacation and come see me. They didn't know yet when they could come, but it would be within the next month or so. Everyone was flying in at once it looked like. I might have a full house, but then there could be a lot of squabbling too. Three Chinese ladies, a Thai girl and a Russian woman: it might be some sort of international incident. I had to wait and see. I might have to disinvite someone, but then more likely no one was coming. I spent every morning chatting with the Thai girl and chatted briefly in the evenings with my Chinese friend and occasionally would email the Russian. Her emails grew much more sporadic and she always questioned me about sex, which I did not mind, but it was a ploy so she could find out what I liked and state how she liked that too. Everything was so transparent.

It turned out I was right. No one came. The Chinese ladies were afraid to stay with a stranger and could not afford a hotel, so that was out. The Russian gal asked me for two thousand dollars the day of her flight, claiming that Customs would not let her get on the plane without the "show money." It was to protect her from being broke when she got to America if her connections failed. I was supposed to wire her the money and then she would return it when she saw me. So, that fell through as well.

That left the Thai girl. She claimed her mother had developed cancer and she had to remain and take care of her. She hurt me the most. I deduced she was just using me for chat and to strengthen her English language skills. English language skills are very marketable in Thailand. So that left me with no one, but just for a brief period. A Finnish woman entered the picture and she was possibly the most beautiful woman I had ever laid eyes on, and we had plenty of sex over the webcam. She stung me for a thousand dollars, and I must have really felt hurt, because I placed a curse on her. I had seen her likeness. I had seen her passport photo, her visa. I knew her real name. I wrote to her in an email, "you will never know comfort or solace in this lifetime." I have every expectation she is a scullery maid now or some babushka that mops floors, even though the latter is a Russian woman.

I needed a wife. I was bound and determined to find someone. I was not playing around. A member of my true family at a concert in 2007 said I was going to get divorced and that I would be alone for three years. She had turned herself into the image of an angel right on the floor of the concert in front of everyone as we spoke. People were aghast. The Finnish girl did not have the proper timing and was attempting to scam anyway, but she got hers. All is fair in love and war. And I am essentially a soldier of both.

Then two old friends entered the picture frame. One was a male and an old friend that I had trusted. It was Christian Bill. He was not a sex partner, never intended to be such, but I needed a friend. I don't shag in that direction and neither does he. I had called him during my divorce and asked him if he would accompany me downtown to an attorney's office, as I was having some trouble thinking and acting rationally. I told him I thought the KGB was after me. He begged off and rightly so. I did not want him to get hurt, but the mere fact that he remembered I found myself in all manner of extreme circumstances made my heart surge with joy. No one had ever understood me like this man. In truth, we had not seen much of each other in the last decade, especially since I had moved to another more distant side of town, but we spoke on the telephone and became confidantes and friends again. I had needed someone, suffering in a sea of silence as I was.

The other friend had more generous and more appealing curves. She was the Marilyn Monroe look alike from my true Internet Don Juan days. And it turned out she lived in an apartment only about five minutes from my house. She emailed me through my website, which I keep primarily for sales of my books, and though she had gone back to her original maiden name, she had called me by her pet name for me. One email I started referring to her as Stinky and she always from then on called me Smelly. So, we struck up a friendship again. She had divorced the abusive husband, and I was without my young Russian beauty queen, but Marilyn and I found our company together was not headed for romance. Still we made fast friends all over again. It became very comfortable to see her most weekends and some evenings.

Christian Bill was busy praying for the end of the world. He wanted to go home, as it were. He considered Heaven his just reward, and a life spent in eternity in bliss all his. He was originally Jewish and very pro Israel, but had converted to Christianity. He swore only true Christians would enter the kingdom of Heaven, and was as devout a holly roller as I had ever seen. He hated gays, Catholics, Muslims, and especially Mormons. He did believe in the rapture and that Christians would be magically carried up to Heaven through the sky when the day arrived. Naturally, he thought that day would be in his lifetime. Florida is actually full of people like this. I think the biggest whackos gravitate to coastal states: the serial killers, the pedophiles, the religious right.

Christian Bill swore that the Jews were going to preemptively attack Iran and knock out its nukes and then clean up matters between the State of Israel and Hezbollah and Syria. He believed the time was closing in that Iran was about to attack Israel and this would start the final battle for the earth, during which the Anti-Christ would appear. It was all biblical prophecy of which he was a staunch believer. But then I had to agree that Israel was likely to let the nukes out. And it was fairly possible that it would be the last country standing in the Middle East. Not that I sympathize. I am not against it either. I don't care. I hate the people of earth. I hate children and pets too. I hope the world does end soon. Then I get to go home that much sooner. And it won't be long at any rate, whether it ends according to the bible or not. So book your accommodations.

I have seen my ship, and it looks cool, so second star on the right and straight on till morning. Except I know I go a little farther away than that. I leave the Milky Way Galaxy and go to the southeast quadrant of the universe. There I own many lands, and many patents, and I am a very wealthy king with three wives. And I fully expect they are not virgins, as that would be kind of boring. And this go round, if they want kids, they can have kids. That is a 180 degrees from how I felt about my peasant wives on earth. My three as I call them are queens of the universe and our sons and daughters will be princes and princesses and handsome and sexy and deliciously bright. And we are time travelers, but after being trapped on earth for so long in the armpit of the universe, which is earth, I am retiring and become a star. And that is my afterlife. My faith. It was revealed to me in 2008 during the time it took me to complete my mission. I mentioned that was about nine months of insanity from December 2007 till August of 2008. I gave birth to myself all over again during that time.

One night I was sitting at home and a voice spoke to me. I had been listening to music and perhaps drinking beer, but there were no drugs involved. That was part of the problem. My medication had failed me. It no longer worked, and I had not yet fully realized. So this voice said, "there is going to be an invasion tonight . . . do you want to fight?"

I said, "I guess so." The voice directed me to start walking. But before I left my house, I grabbed two thousand dollars I had taken from my checking account earlier that day at the behest of another voice. There was so much going on in my life, and with my mind, I am surprised my brains did not leak out of my ears. So, I grabbed my money and put it in my wallet and took off down the street on foot. The voice that had mentioned the invasion said turn right. I turned right. It said there is a gas station farther down. I said out loud that I knew it. "Go there and await your orders." It was clear to me I was a soldier for some cosmic good, Luke Skywalker, and I would follow orders. My mission of a series of missions was about to commence.

As I walked along to the gas station, freaky things started happening. It appeared certain gangs of people in cars were looking for me, and though I was right out in the open, they could not find me. They would say, "no, that's not him . . ." I walked along and guessed I was changing form, but it was not at my will. I did not have any control over it. It was to make me unrecognizable. The gangs kept calling out to me and pleading with me not to do what I was about to do. I arrived at the gas station. A voice said call a taxi.

I asked some grizzled man working at the gas station if he would call a taxi for me. He said there was a pay phone on the pole. There are very few public pay phones left in Tampa. But sure enough, there was one there. I asked him for a phone book, which he provided, if somewhat ungraciously. My mind was tense. I could not comprehend the phonebook. I asked the grizzled and haggard looking man if he would look up a number for a cab company. He did so. I then asked him if he would write it down for me. Normally, I would never have required all this attention. He wrote down the number. But I had no change for the telephone. I only had bills, so I bought a coke and received change for the pay phone. It took some doing, but I placed the call. The taxi arrived within ten minutes. It was as if it had been waiting for me.

It had leather seats and the cabbie was playing loud rock and roll music. I smiled at him and he smiled back. I climbed in the backseat and we were off. He pulled into traffic and the aliens following me lost my trail. I settled down a bit. He asked, "where to?" I said, "can you take me to San Diego for two thousand dollars?" He said, "I think so, but I have to check with my boss."

He took me to the airport where his boss was. It was crowded. I thought I might be getting on a plane, but I had no bags, and I knew I could not get through Security in this state of mind. I was clearly agitated. It was 2008, not pre 9/11. Plus a ticket would be expensive and I had to fight a war, so that meant I was fighting ground troops as best I could tell. The aliens working for the CIA were communicating with me telepathically. I could even hear the voice of a former president. The former president did not want to see me succeed. He communicated with me telepathically as well, as he was also an alien. I wonder how many presidents have been? The voices were swirling around my head. I also heard my family's voices. Not my earth mother and brother and sisters, even though they were also aliens. I had defeated them. I had earned the right to be left alone by them. They were mostly witches and my brother was either a warlock or a warlord. Peasants. They were not Immortals as I am.

So we got to the airport.

The cabbie stepped out of his cab and found his boss. I was carrying on a conversation out loud with the multitude of voices in my head. I heard the cabbie's boss say, "he's talking to himself." To which I replied from inside the cab, "I am schizophrenic. I have some business in San Diego, and then I am taking a plane back home." The boss gave his blessing, and we were headed back into town to pick up I-75 and head north. The worst fighting was along I-75; in fact, all of it was. Every big rig on the highway was carrying armament meant to destroy me. The aliens had called out the big guns, but I was up to the battle. Here and there I skillfully manipulated my cigarette like a Chinese throwing star, sticking it in the right eye of my opponent. It went in their right eye because the left eye is reserved for ranking aliens, and I outranked them all. I am a king of many lands. I am an Immortal. I go to the southeast quadrant of the universe and set up residence after this life with three wives. And I am not Mormon. I follow no organized religion. Others may follow me, but my following days are done. In the next life, I claim my prize.

The cabbie belted rock and roll songs from his stereo. In the heat of battle Queen's *"Bohemian Rhapsody"* came on and I made short work, mopping up the aliens and frying their vehicles and leaving thousands of trucks stranded along I-75. It looked like something from a Day After movie. I would hit my hand against the glass and say, "normal" and the lights would fail on these huge rigs, pouring in from all over to try and get a shot off at me. When their lights went out, it meant they had no power and no more fighter capabilities. They were just regular trucks. They were driving into Tampa on I-75 South, and I was shooting at them with my cigarettes, "ten kill, twenty kill, fifty kill power" from across the interstate. They were taken completely by surprise. Sacked. My Trojan horse had fooled them all.

The biggest of the big rigs, at least a few of them with superior technology, were regenerating. They took their second wave of power from phone lines and possibly satellites put up in space by alien forces. That is when the moon got in on the act. I felt the hand of God again in my life. The moon said, "let me play." I said, "okay." The moon fried the power lines and caught the trucks on fire. They piled up on the side of the road. It was a death waltz. A former president was infuriated. He threatened to have me incarcerated. God had told me I would never be a prisoner again, so I laughed. The Pleaidean army was defeated. I had saved earth a second or possibly third time. I honestly lost count.

All was good in my life. I had successfully completed my mission or missions on earth. It had been a long time coming. I never thought, one that I would live to be such an age with all the various attempts against my life, and two that I would have the energy to fight like I did so late in my life, but I was in full possession of my faculties. I had defeated an invading army, and while it may not have been singlehandedly, I did not have that much help. But then I knew from the start I could not fail. My true family would never set me up to fail. So after a period in an alien lockdown around Tallahassee, I escaped and found my way home. My house was as I had left it. The kitchen had been cleaned. I assumed my mother had let herself in. She turned out to be a useful alien to know. She had had my back several times before. I will miss her when she reforms. She will not die. More likely she will go to another part of the universe.

With my mission completed, I figured no better time than to leave this planet. So I attempted to overdose on about six vials of pills, but I failed. My mother broke into my house and called the EMT's and they took me to the hospital where I lay in a coma for three nights. After this part of the saga is when I rebuilt my life and began my serial dating again. I met a Raelian woman. Raelianism is an extra-terrestrial religion, fairly new, which professes free love, something like the hippies of the 60's and 70's. They are rather odd people, but I found this woman entertaining and easily orgasmic. She was nothing special to look at, but she would drive in and have sex with me and spend the weekend with me, which was a pleasant diversion.

I was also back at work by this time. I am a college professor by trade, but I never date my students. At any rate I switched to another college so I could cash out my 403b, because I needed money. Why Congress passed that law that you had to quit a job to access those funds is quite beyond me. I hate politicians. They are all Shitheads nowadays. But I did quit my job, and found a new one soon enough after. This particular college was a technical school, so the students were primarily males, which worked out well, as I was still vulnerable and might have tried dating a student, which is usually frowned upon. So I had my disability and my job and my savings, and I could mostly afford my bills once again.

Then my mother moved in with me, which presented some difficulties at first. She is very a strong-willed woman, bossy to say the least, and as I had just saved the earth, I was not likely to listen to anyone about anything. I had done my service. She was quite elderly, but also quite pushy and an angry individual and stubborn, and she vented her rage by weeping often. Guilt was a favorite weapon too, but I am somewhat impervious to it. I was usually respectful, and I owned a large house, so she would read and watch television a bit and sit out by the pool, and I could do things as I liked. I missed playing my music loud. And I wanted to be left alone and work, but she could never allow me that either. Then she had a heart attack. But I could not tell her to do anything. After all at this age she was 89 years old. And she had become a child again. It really is true what Shakespeare says: the seven stages of life. In the end we are all infants again, sans teeth.

My mother put quite a crimp in my activities. She did not recover from her heart attack immediately. I had to do all of the cooking and cleaning, which I was accustomed to when living by myself, but I did not like picking up after someone else, not even my mother. I had to do all the grocery shopping and run her up to the library if she could get out. My mother had loved to get out and drive her Saturn. She had a boyfriend that lived about ninety miles south and they would meet in a coastal community. Alas, she had to give up driving for a time, but in my special heart of hearts, I knew she would recover. I could tell.

My father had never wanted to be a burden, as my first wife and I had offered for him to live with us. But then my mother was not a burden either. It just took some life rearranging. But the lifestyle rearranging was all on my part, as she was quite unwilling or incapable of doing anything of the such at her age. It is difficult living with family; more so, it is difficult living with them when all members in the home are adults. Most of the time I enjoyed having my mother around, but the house had grown so quiet and still. It had the feeling of a morgue like the juices were being sucked out. It had been a lively house when my second wife and I moved in. Now, it plodded along, same day stretching into same day, no excitement, no fun, just work and chores. I began to hate my life.

Then one night I had the most amazing dream. I had worked late into the night. I had taught a composition class and did not get home until after ten pm. Then I ate dinner and graded papers and watched a little television. When I finally turned in after one am, I was awakened by a searing pain in my left eye. It was a holdover from my cosmic warrior days. The Shitheads sought to blind me, so they loaded up my left eye with as much crap as they could. The Shitheads could actually sling crap into one's eyes. I was the ranking officer, so it had to go in my left eye. The underlings take it in their right eye. The doctors stated it was just severely dry eyes. Most of the doctors and attorneys are Shitheads now.

This dream had the potential to make me the wealthiest man ever in earth's history. The end of the dream caught me by surprise. I was looking up into the sky with a relatively small number of people, maybe six or eight, and saw something truly disturbing. It was images of items projected against the clouds. Some were of an eye, others a house with a fire burning in the fireplace, and some more bizarre and unrecognizable. It was alien technology and seemed threatening. I interpreted the images to mean we had been invaded again, and this time would be enslaved, because our masters had far superior technology. I was scared. This dream came sort of as a nightmare. Perhaps the spicy beef I ate before sleep, or ruminations over not my best performance in class were getting to me. Then at the end of the dream, up popped the Pizza Hut logo.

It was all a marketing tool ala something akin to the Bat Signal. And I knew I could cash in. I own a refinement of this very same patent in the quadrant of the universe I go to next, and it promotes robust sales for our quadrant and the southwest quadrant of the universe, who are our trading partners. It is the source of some major bank accounts, and the secret of how it operates is kept well under wraps. So on earth, I have no way to patent this tool, which is a laser that projects 3D holographic images against some type of background in the sky.

It was day time during my dream, but I am sure some clever geek could transform the technology so it could work at night as well. Maybe all that would be needed for that would be a source of light like a large flood light. I can't say which is worse, neon signs or advertising on clouds. But as soon as someone figures a way on earth to do just that, he will make potentially billions. In one week, it will be everywhere. Imagine walking out of your front door and being bombarded with commercials playing on the clouds. I find that notion horrific and want to go home more now than ever. But if I can cash in on it, I might not be so upset. Maybe we could have and carry remote controls for the clouds. Cloud changers.

If you don't like the show or commercial, change it to another laser system. Cable cloud systems. The messages could be personalized for each individual, reminder notes of what to pick up at the store or traveling directions or one's favorite dramas or comedies to watch. It would include the next wave of cellular technology and GPS. And it would be high definition in 3D.

We could tune in the audio by way of satellite radio or over our blue tooths. Or perhaps just some crappy AM station. We would have instant access to everything when we were out. Some clever marketing agency will put the right spin on it, and it is coming. I guar-an-tee! We are moving down the path of the virtual world anyway. What is one more step. Granted what I am talking about here is a big step, but before long in the next good economy, everyone will have this technology at his or her beck and call. America will sell it to the Chinese who will make a cheaper knockoff version and it will spread like wildfire. Meanwhile, Bill Gates step aside. What a hack he will seem! He will be out of money by then anyway.

There was another ray of sunshine as well. Mai. She is the niece of the husband of my manicurist and from Vietnam. My manicurist had been a Buddhist Priestess. She converted to Christianity when she came to the United States, but Mai was still in Saigon or Ho Chi Minh City, as it was renamed. My manicurist had an English name because she had been educated in English schools, and went by the name Angela. How she became a Buddhist Priestess is a bit of a mystery to me. Angela had three-way calling on her cell phone, and she could call Vietnam for free as she still had numerous relatives there. So I would get to talk to Mai any time I dropped by Angela's work. Angela worked as a nail technician in another man's shop. At first the conversations were difficult, as Mai could not say much, but I could tell she was a smart girl. She worked very hard every day and we could also email each other. She would clean and cook and make my bed and bring in an income. She was divorced, which was considered rare in Vietnamese society and she had one child, but her son would not be coming with her.

The best part of the deal was that Angela had stated she would bring Mai. I would not have to pay anything until Mai and I were married. But then I got enlisted in running Angela's husband around to the doctor and the various pharmacies. He had asthma and a heart condition. But Mai was very cute, slender about five foot nothing, maybe a hundred and ten pounds. She had shoulder length black hair and a little, flat nose and a round chin. She was slated to come in October, but I wondered if it would be more like December. A member of my true family had told me at the Blue Man Group concert just before my second wife left me that I would be alone for three years. The concert was in November 2007 and my wife committed her last little indiscretion in December 2007, and it would be December 2010 before I found another partner. At this point in my narrative as I write this that time fast approaches.

Mai would tell me she loved me and that she was very happy. She would say, "I work every day." Vietnamese women are usually submissive, so as I am a switch and can be dominant or submissive, that all seemed fine with me. We became engaged. Everyone else had sort of run the course and fizzled out. So here I was engaged again, and once again to someone I had not met and that lived overseas. That would not stop me from playing. I did not have a lot of confidence that Angela knew what she was doing and could successfully bring Mai. She might pull it off, but I would keep looking in the meantime. So, I more or less kept up my serial dating efforts. I found sex partners, nice girls, scammers, and some hopeless cases. There is everything in this world and plenty of it, especially on the Internet.

My mother in the meantime drove me crazier and crazier. I was convinced her hormones were whacked out. She would weep for any little reason. She secretly hated her children though she stood by each and every one of them. She could never confess this, especially not to herself, but it was true. We had kept her from having her grand business career because she had to take care of us because our father was such a flake and wound up traipsing around the planet with a younger woman. My stepmother was an alcoholic that committed suicide. I did not have a lot of respect for her. I did not know exactly if my mother's tears were tears of manipulation or bonafide and the result of some internal chemistry problem.

As I said my mother missed her calling in every aspect of her life. She should have been Jewish. She wielded guilt as expertly as any Jewish mother. I called them my mother's moods of mass destruction. And she never stopped bossing. She thought of me as a child, and I hated her for that. I used to fantasize about having roommates, but I knew I would never ask my mother to leave again. She had bailed me out when I was sick and working for the CIA, which organization owed me a lot of money that I guessed I would never see. I was so desperate during this time I considered buying a gun and just keeping it if I ever wanted to turn off the lights.

Meanwhile, I kept teaching. In the government's infinite wisdom, it raised the amount that those on disability could earn each month, which meant I could teach a second class without penalty. I would have a little more cash, and this was during a time when the economy was the worst I had ever seen it. My mother commented it had never been this bad in her lifetime since 1933. She had grown up on a farm in East St. Louis and her family had food, and could barter for whatever else it needed. Every night she told me, men would come to the backdoor and her mother, my grandmother, would carry out plates of fried chicken and biscuits and milk. They may have saved thousands of lives.

Teaching had gotten to be a bit of a ridiculous profession, owing to corporate schools and grade inflation in part, but a teacher could not afford to piss off a student. Shots fired on high school and college campuses were routine, and while tragic, they barely went noticed anymore. It did not pay to anger students, who had become a very rough and tumble bunch or college administrations that were bent on profits and made money off federal financial aid. So, students grade grubbed as much as they saw fit. They needed to graduate with a 4.0 to get in another program or get an advanced degree. It became easier to give it to them. I realized the students I was toughest on would appreciate it most in the long run, and I was always as fair as I could be, but it no longer paid to push students in the kind of schools I now found myself working. Those that were disciplined enough would have to push themselves, and many of them did. At any rate, I had taught for over twenty years and I was not an idealistic child just starting out.

Then I received the email that changed my life. Or at least I thought it would change my life.

Chapter Three

Nicoletta wrote me. She had been my first choice all this time. Since her last email maybe a year had gone by. She wrote, "my love, it is time to tell you the truth of why I did not come. My father beat my mom horribly, and I stayed with her in her hospital room until she died. Then there was a trial, and my father received life behind bars." The email was written in very good English, but then Nicole was an educated girl and had good English. "Then I went crazy. I stayed in hospital for a time, but now have fully recovered. I didn't think it could happen to me. I lost my mind. And if you still want me, I am ready to come. I just need $300 to change my ticket." There was the rub. She was asking for money again; money I had sent her once. And at that time, it was a tough economy and $300 was not easy to come by. But I sent her the money, at least $200 of it. She said she could raise the other $100. Again. I had to see my investment all the way through to the bitter end. If she came, we would get married. If not, I was out an additional $200, but still had the Vietnamese girl coming soon.

I had grown to despise my life being so alone and lonely, and taking care of my unforgiving mother. My mother was desperately afraid of being alone and not having someone's life to orchestrate. Without being in charge of someone else's life, she felt she had no purpose. My life punished me, and all I had ever done was live it. My heart went out to Mai, the Vietnamese woman, if Nicole did arrive. She would be without a man, but her family was resourceful and could hook her up with someone. Communication between the two of us was scant anyway. And her English was poor. Even six months later after we began initially talking by telephone, she could say only the same limited things. She could say, "I work every day," and "I love you, darling." My buddy Bill said that reminded him of an Asian hooker he had known. "I love you long time, darling."

There came another wrinkle in the Internet Don Juan's life. It involved some sort of investigation by Interpol and I am sketchy on the details. A man with the same first and last name of the Finnish beauty who scammed me joined my social networking page on a popular website. I use social networking sites to promote my books. I immediately responded to his request and approved it. I then asked him where my fucking money was. His photo was that of a man too young to be the Finnish beauty's father, but I guessed he was her husband. I knew she had a male partner, and she had pawned it off as though this person was her father. I could tell from the chat dialogues we had there was an older male involved. This other man with the same name actually came on chat on the social networking site with me. I told him he and his wife had ripped me off, but he protested. I was pretty hot with him, and I threatened him, and I told him I knew where he lived in Finland and I would send someone to get him and his lovely wife.

It turned out the man was an investigator for Interpol, the international crime fighting association. I had given him my city and my email address to let me know what the control number was, so I could pick my money up via Western Union, because I demanded he pay me back. I figured I would never hear from him again. But the next day he sent me an email which included a photo of a woman and asked if this was the woman who scammed me. I said no. The woman who scammed me had bigger breasts and darker hair. So then he claimed he got a photo off the Internet and asked if she was the one. It was she. I'll never forget those soulful brown eyes. He included an attachment of his badge, and it looked legitimate, so I assumed perhaps this woman was going to be brought to justice. The gentleman and I traded emails for the better part of a day, and he was convinced this woman had been involved in various Internet scams and began building a case, as he said. "Vengeance is mine, saith the Lord." I have always interpreted that phrase from the Bible personally. I am not some Holy Roller, but this woman had gotten the better of me, so turnabout is fair play.

I had sent the $200 to Nicole. Then no word. Finally, I got a short email saying her travel agent was out of town the month of August. It was at the beginning of August and I would have to wait. She claimed to be very distraught. I took it in stride. She was a long shot. She always had been. Various dating websites would have free communication weekends as they put it. I would join and maybe meet one or two people, but the local girls did not do it for me. I liked the import models. I still had a fancy house that was nearly paid for and a sports car, but no money in the bank. It was a house of cards. I still wanted Nicole. And I did not want to settle for the Vietnamese girl, who might have made a suitable partner, but she was experiencing visa problems. It seemed the government did not want a young Vietnamese girl to come to America. She was by then 30 years old, and not a child, but the government had this habit of squarely intervening in my life and I hated it. Governments rot. All of them.

All this time I had been chatting with another amazing beauty. She was from Mexico City and worked as a financial controller, but was currently out of work. She was thirty-nine and had no children and had never been married. I had slipped up once and told her she was the third heiress to the crown, meaning if Romania and Vietnam could not get their respective acts together I would marry this woman from Mexico. I always wanted a wife from North America, my first being Middle Eastern and my second being Eastern European. Well, Maria did not take the news well that there were two women ahead of her and I had to see how they played out first. But on Maria's fortieth birthday they had both played out, so I invited Maria to come visit, so we could contemplate marriage.

She owned a house and a car and had worked for most of her life for American companies. That was a plus. I knew I could find her a job in my hometown. She wanted to work again, but had been displaced because of the worldwide economic issues. Mexico City is a city of approximately twenty-five million. I was there with friends and family in 2004. It is a spectacular place. Maria grabbed a flight into Miami from where I picked her up, and the timing could not have been more perfect. I had two weeks summer vacation from my teaching duties. We spent the night at a hotel in South Beach and played on the beach and sipped coffee at a café, and then drove home. Maria was impressed with Florida and the ride was pleasant. She dozed a bit, and I listened to the stereo.

I think Maria was finally ready to start a new life. Mexico had more or less played out for her. She felt the Mexican government did not do enough for its people. She could not find a job there, and though her house was paid for and she could afford to live, she did not exactly live a luxurious life. She rented her house to her sister, and sold her car, after visiting the first time. She spent two weeks with me in my home the first visit. We played in the pool and made love every night. We went out to the beach and had coffee. It was all a very pleasant routine, and I could see I had finally found my latest soul mate. We were married in December of 2010, and finally the Don Juan's days were put behind him. For good, I hoped. It was my third marriage, and Maria's first, and I knew she would stick around and make it work, as would I. No more divorces for the Don.

She had good English, which had attracted me initially. I taught her how to cook, and we prepared some fabulous meals together. We met some other couples and entertained at our house. I was true to my promise and found her a job as an accountant with an insurance company, making good money. She was thrilled and decided to sit for her CPA exam, which she passed the first time. Then she got a big promotion, and we went car shopping for her. She was good at saving money, so we had enough always to get by. And we visited her sister in Mexico City a couple of times. The Museo de Anthropologia is a complete fascination to me. It is the world's premier Anthropological museum.

So, everything worked out after all. I had been told by a true family member, the girl at the Blue Man Group concert, that I would be alone for three years, and I was. It was the fall of the third year and then into winter that I met and married my senorita. She has this delicious accent, she is dynamite in the bedroom, and we make a happy pair. I am thrilled. My mother is still alive and lives with us. My wife and mother get along well. It takes a great deal of the pressure off me. I feel like I have a family again, not to mention my overseas relatives in Mexico, who adore me. It has all worked out for me. I am lucky. Persistent, but more lucky. And I have a great gal as my reward.

So Don Juan gets on his horse, lifts a hand to his woman, and helps her on behind him, and they ride off into the sunset.